"I'm really looking forward to Bitsy's party. It's my only chance to see everyone before leaving for college." Nicole sounded both happy and sad.

"Really?" Cindy bit her lip. Nicole would be shocked to know that Bitsy wasn't the only one planning a farewell party. Nicole's party would be a total surprise. Enjoying her secret, Cindy continued, "I don't know—maybe Bitsy's making too much of a fuss about graduation."

Nicole raised her eyebrows in a superior manner. "You just don't understand. Wait until you have to leave your oldest friends behind."

"Big deal," Cindy teased, thinking of all the friends who'd be at Nicole's party. "I'd be too excited about the future to worry about the past."

"It *is* a big deal," Nicole said seriously.

"Hey, Nicole, lighten up. I was kidding," Cindy assured her. "Of course I'd miss my old friends if I were going away. Anybody would be crazy not to."

"But, making new friends . . ." Nicole hesitated. "Do you think it's harder in college?"

The SISTERS Series
by Jennifer Cole
Published by Fawcett Girls Only Books:

Other titles in the Girls Only series
available upon request

SISTERS

COLLEGE
BOUND

Jennifer Cole

FAWCETT GIRLS ONLY • NEW YORK

RLI: $\dfrac{\text{VL 5 \& up}}{\text{IL 6 \& up}}$

A Fawcett Girls Only Book
Published by Ballantine Books
Copyright © 1988 by Cloverdale Press, Inc.

Library of Congress Catalog Card Number: 87-92124

ISBN 0-449-13493-8

Manufactured in the United States of America

First Edition: August 1988

Chapter 1

*N*icole Lewis, *her usually neat brown hair* drooping in a messy ponytail, glanced at her younger sister. Mollie stood in the doorway of Nicole's bedroom, her blue eyes wide in surprise.

"What are you looking at?" Nicole demanded. For goodness' sake, didn't Mollie realize she had packing to do?

Mollie's mouth dropped open. "Nicole, you aren't dressed!"

"I already knew that," Nicole replied impatiently.

"But it's lunchtime."

"It is not."

"It is!"

"It couldn't be," Nicole protested. She checked her wristwatch. Mollie was right—it was well past noon, and late for anyone in the Lewis family to be lounging about in pajamas and a bathrobe.

Mollie drew closer. "Are you sick?"

1

"No, Mollie. I'm fine. *Laisse-moi*," Nicole grumbled in French.

Because Nicole was famous for mixing in a little French with her English, Mollie took no notice. Besides, she had no idea that *laisse-moi* meant "leave me alone." She plopped on the foot of Nicole's bed—the only bare patch in the room, as far as she could tell.

"You're not dressed, your hair's a complete mess—and your room is a disaster area," Mollie pronounced in a tone of disbelief.

"*Certainement.* I'm busy," Nicole said crossly. She suppressed an urge to boot her inquisitive little sister out of the room. But after all, in only a few days—Nicole drew a steadying breath—she'd be in a college dormitory, with no little sisters to annoy her.

"Packing for college must be worse than I thought," Mollie remarked. "I've never see Nicole Lewis so disorganized before."

"I am *not* disorganized," Nicole snapped, turning her attention back to the pile of clothes in front of her.

"Okay, okay—I get the hint," Mollie said quickly. "I'm going." She got up and retreated to the door.

Meanwhile Nicole rolled her bulky ski sweater into a ball and tried to cram it into an already overstuffed suitcase. The hard vinyl lid refused to shut. "*Mon Dieu*," she cried in exasperation as the lid sprang up in her face.

Mollie hesitated. "Uh, maybe I could help," she offered. "Let me."

Nicole shrugged and reluctantly handed over her sweater.

"If you lay it flat, like this, everything will fit." Carefully Mollie arranged the sweater on top of the clothes in the suitcase, closed the lid, clicked the locks shut, and stood back, a look of satisfaction on her face. "But why not pack sweaters in your trunk?" she asked sensibly.

Nicole gave a frustrated cry and leaned her head in her hands. "*Je ne sais pas!* I can't think straight this morning."

"You're too hyped up," Mollie said, very wisely for her fourteen years. "But I suppose I would be too, if I were going off on my own in a few days."

Nicole stared at her sister. Mollie was absolutely right. She *was* too hyped up to think straight. In fact, her head ached terribly. She hadn't slept well at all the night before. Every time she thought about leaving home, her excitement about going to college faded. Instead, she felt an awful hollowness in the pit of her stomach. But she could hardly admit that to Mollie. As the eldest Lewis sister, Nicole felt obligated to set the right example for Mollie and sixteen-year-old Cindy.

Carefully, Nicole put on a slightly disinterested expression. "I don't know what you mean about being hyped up, Mollie. I happen to be perfectly calm," she said. Shaking her hair loose from the ponytail, she forced herself to sit at her dressing table. *Quel désastre*, she thought, looking at her reflection in the mirror. I am a mess!

Behind her, Mollie sorted idly through the clothes strewn over the bed. "Are you making piles of clothes to take to the dry cleaner's?"

"Those are shirts that don't match any outfits." Brushing her hair vigorously, Nicole was starting to feel more like herself. She shouldn't have stayed in her robe so long; she felt all out of sorts. And the chaos of her room was driving her crazy. She hadn't meant to start packing at all that morning. She had only wondered how much she could fit in her suitcase. But somehow she had ended up with all her clothes pulled out of drawers and closets, and when she tried to pack them away, she only succeeded in making things worse.

She sighed. Mollie was right; she was too hyped up. Instead of looking forward to college, she was actually starting to dread it.

"You're crazy," Mollie cried.

"What?" Nicole started. Was Mollie reading her mind?

"About these shirts—" Mollie held up a discarded shirt and one of Nicole's sweaters—"they match your outfits. Look at this."

Nicole frowned. "That's a striped shirt and a flowered sweater."

"Yes." Mollie nodded patiently as if talking to a child, "but the colors are exactly the same. See—they look great together."

Again Mollie was right. The shirt and sweater did match well. Nicole never would have thought of combining different patterns as Mollie had.

"And this!" Excitedly Mollie pulled a crumpled skirt from the bed. "This is terrific."

"That old thing?" Nicole shrugged. "I've never liked it. And it's too long for this year. Out of fashion."

Mollie rolled her eyes. "Really, Nicole, I thought you had style. Put this skirt with your tall boots and that turtleneck sweater—perfect! It's even French-looking."

Nicole nodded, pretending to be more interested in her hair than her old skirt. Mollie happened to be right once again, but Nicole wasn't used to taking advice from her little sister. She hated to admit that Mollie knew better than she did about anything, even about something as silly as matching skirts and sweaters.

Acting the part of the slightly superior college student, Nicole continued dressing, keeping one eye on Mollie, who was cheerfully separating her clothes into neat piles.

"*Mon Dieu*, Mollie, now I won't know where anything is," she exclaimed.

"Sure you will. Everything is in order. Look." Mollie gestured to the clothes in front of her. "This pile is casual things to wear to classes," she explained, "and that pile is dressier stuff, like for parties or dates." She held up a pale green silk blouse, pairing it with an off-white suit that Nicole had thought of giving away.

"I'm probably not keeping that suit," Nicole said.

Mollie's blue eyes widened. "But it's perfect for your freshman dinner, isn't it? I mean, I thought so."

"*Peut-être*. Maybe," Nicole said, mentally erasing one item off her mile-long list of problems.

Two weeks before, she had received her freshman information pack from Briarwood College. Included was a detailed list of activities planned for Freshman Orientation Week. The highlight was to be a formal dinner where the incoming class would meet the college president. Nicole had been agonizing over what to wear to the dinner and had just about decided that she'd have to buy something special at school. Nothing she owned had seemed appropriate. But now Mollie had put together the perfect outfit. One she'd had all the time, if only she'd stopped to think.

"And these leggings are great for football games," Mollie enthused. "Wear them with any of your long sweaters."

"All right, all right." Nicole sighed. "You've convinced me. I'll keep everything." She pulled on her favorite jeans.

"Well, not everything." Mollie pointed to a stack of clothes on the rug. "You never even wear those, so maybe . . ."

"I get the hint. Okay, they're yours."

Mollie's face broke into a happy smile. "You mean it? I always loved that yellow outfit, but you never, ever wore it. . . ."

"I said they're yours. Those and that stuff in my closet, at the end. Even you couldn't find matches for those."

Mollie flew to the closet and immediately started trying on ·Nicole's discards, oohing and aahing over her new treasures.

"This is great," she said. "I can't believe it. You should go away more often." She caught Nicole's eye. "Only kidding," she assured her sister lightly.

Nicole turned away. Not for one minute has Mollie acted sad that I'm leaving home, Nicole thought. Instead, she's excited about getting these dumb hand-me-downs. She doesn't really care if I'm here or not—she just cares about my clothes.

Mollie sighed rapturously. "Just think, Nicole—football games, cheering for your own college team. It's so romantic. And think of the dances and fraternity parties and dates—I wish I was going to college. You're so lucky to be eighteen already and on your own."

Nicole smiled weakly. "I know."

"Wouldn't you love to get your own apartment?" Mollie asked dreamily.

"Maybe," Nicole said.

"Definitely," Mollie insisted. "Maybe not your first semester, though. You'll make more friends in the dorm. But later you could have your very own place—all to yourself. I can just imagine it!"

Mollie's eyes shone with excitement, but Nicole shifted her own eyes away. The more excited Mollie got, the less excited Nicole felt.

"Are you okay?" Mollie was eyeing her curiously.

"Naturellement." Nicole tossed her head.

Since junior year of high school she and her friends had talked endlessly about college. Nicole had been thrilled with the prospect of being on her own, and going East had been most thrilling of all.

Not that Nicole didn't love California, and especially her home town. Santa Barbara was beautiful. With the mountains on one side and the ocean on the other, and lots of cultural events happening right in town, Santa Barbara had just about everything. Still, when she'd planned on college, Nicole had been dazzled by the history and tradition of the big eastern schools. Getting accepted at Briarwood College in Massachusetts had been a dream come true. Until now—now that she was actually *going*.

Nicole's gaze wandered around the room, finally resting on a picture pinned to her bulletin board. Thoughtfully she took the snapshot down to have a closer look. "Mollie—remember this? The Château Frontenac in Quebec. Wasn't it beautiful?"

Mollie barely glanced at the photo. "Oh, sure. Where's that sweatshirt?" she muttered.

The three Lewis sisters had recently spent several weeks in Quebec, staying with an old friend of their mother's. While Cindy had conquered the local hockey rink and Mollie had immediately fallen head-over-heels in love, Nicole had struggled with a special honors course in French. For the first time in her life Nicole hadn't been at the top of the class. She'd had a lot of trouble just passing the course, and it had been an unsettling experience. The knot in her stomach now was similar to the one she'd had in Quebec, facing that class each day. The fact that she had been more homesick than either Cindy or Mollie hadn't helped, either.

Carefully Nicole replaced the snapshot. Those weeks in Quebec had seemed like years, and now she was going away for real. I don't know if I'm ready to leave home, she thought. I guess I'm not as grown up as I like to think I am. The knot in her stomach grew tighter. What if I get to college and can't make it on my own?

"Nicole," Mollie was saying, "do you agree? I'll swap you my blue sweatshirt for this green one. It's brand new, and it goes with everything you own."

"*Oui, oui, certainement,*" Nicole muttered vaguely.

Looking around, she realized that the clutter had disappeared. Her room was neat and orderly again. "Mollie—what did you do?" She gaped in surprise.

Mollie gave a smug grin. "I put things away for you." She opened a bureau drawer. "Everything in the bottom is for taking with you," she explained. "The stuff in your closet will go in your trunk, and this"—she pointed to the extra set of clothes left on the bed—"is to take on the plane in your flight bag, in case your luggage gets lost."

Impressed, Nicole just nodded. Obviously Mollie hadn't forgotten the disaster in Canada, when the sisters had missed their connecting flight and Mollie had gotten stuck without any luggage, with no clean clothes or underwear, or even so much as a toothbrush.

"*Merci,*" Nicole said weakly.

"I wish I was going to college," Mollie declared. "It's so glamorous—living in a brand new town. All the fabulous sophisticated guys back East! I know—" Mollie snatched up Nicole's makeup case "—let's give you a whole new look. We want you to make an instant impression. So you'll get the best guys before any other girl does."

Nicole grabbed the makeup case away. "Do you mind?" she asked curtly. "I think I know how to put my own makeup on."

"I was only trying to help, Nicole."

"I don't need any more help. I can do some things myself."

"Okay, okay." Rolling her eyes, Mollie backed

toward the door. "Boy, you try to be nice to some people!"

Nicole felt like slamming the door, but she waited for Mollie to disappear before closing it calmly. The truth was, Mollie was *too* helpful. It made Nicole feel as though she should be the younger sister. Actually, that wouldn't be so bad, Nicole mused. If I were the younger sister, I wouldn't be getting ready to leave home.

With surprise Nicole felt tears well up in her eyes. For an instant she wished she were staying home and not going away to college at all. She shook her head impatiently. What was wrong with her? She felt like running after Mollie and holding on to her little sister. Wouldn't that be a switch, Nicole thought with a sniffle. I'm the one Mollie usually runs to for comfort.

Carefully Nicole dried her eyes and smoothed on some lipstick. It wouldn't do to let anyone see her this way. Grabbing her freshman information pack, she hurried downstairs.

Chapter 2

*D*ownstairs, *the table was already set for lunch.*
Laura Lewis was at the kitchen counter putting
the finishing touches on a luncheon salad of tossed
meats, pasta, and vegetables. Winston, the family
dog, begged at her heels.

"Not now, Winston," Mrs. Lewis told the huge
Newfoundland, "no begging allowed. Whose turn
is it to feed him?"

Nicole hurried into the room. "Sorry—it's my
turn." Tossing her freshman information pack onto
the counter stool, Nicole grabbed a can of dog
food from the cupboard and quickly emptied it
into Winston's bowl.

"The cats, too," Mrs. Lewis reminded her gently.

Mr. Lewis pulled out a chair for his wife. "We
missed you at breakfast, Nicole."

"Oh—I, uh, slept late," Nicole replied.

"Don't apologize—it's just that I enjoy a family
breakfast now and then. Especially on a Sunday,

when your mother has the day off, too—which is rare enough, nowadays."

Nicole frowned. "Your day off. I'm sorry, Mother. I would have made lunch for us."

"I don't mind, Nicole."

"But I promised, your next day off you weren't supposed to cook." Nicole grew thoughtful. "I know—let me make dinner tonight instead."

Laura Lewis smiled delightedly. "I accept. Your father and I just got last-minute tickets to a play at the Civic Center—if you make dinner, we'll have more time to get ready."

"*Bon*. Then, it's settled." Relieved, Nicole dug into her lunch. She was pleased to be a help to her mother. Mrs. Lewis's catering business, Moveable Feasts, was doing so well lately that they hardly saw her at all. When she was home, their mother was often exhausted from the hard work of running the business. Nicole chewed thoughtfully. Her mother really could use some extra help at Moveable Feasts—another full-time employee, or even an assistant manager.

"Mother, Moveable Feasts is doing really well, isn't it?"

"Why, yes, dear. Better than I ever dreamed."

"Well, I just wondered ..." Nicole hesitated. "Maybe you should expand the business."

"I'm spread thin enough as it is." Mrs. Lewis accepted a second helping of salad from Cindy.

"*Oui, je sais*. I know," Nicole continued, "but suppose I were to stay home this year and help out? Maybe you could open a second shop. I've heard you and Dad discuss the idea."

Cindy's mouth dropped open, and Mollie was

so startled, she dropped half a piece of bread onto the table, butter side down.

"Stay home!" Mollie gasped. "Are you crazy?"

Cindy tilted her chair back, a skeptical look on her suntanned face. "Is this my sister Nicole—the one who's been ranting and raving all her life about going away to some eastern school?"

Nicole felt herself flush. "I'm just trying to help out," she protested. "Neither of you cares how hard mother works."

"We do, too!" Indignantly Mollie slapped her fork down. "I help whenever I'm asked."

"Some help." Cindy grinned. "You don't know a soufflé from scrambled eggs."

"You should talk," Mollie protested, tossing her long blond hair behind her. "You cook the way you surf. . . ."

"Girls, please!" Mr. Lewis held up a hand for order.

Quizzically, Mrs. Lewis eyed Nicole. "Honey, it's sweet of you to offer, but I wouldn't dream of accepting."

Nicole bit her lip. "It was just an idea."

"A very nice idea, but nothing is more important to me than having you start school, just as you planned."

"Absolutely," Mr. Lewis agreed. "Your mother is right. College is much too important to postpone."

"I only thought . . ."

Mrs. Lewis laid a hand over Nicole's, squeezing it fondly. "Thank you, Nicole, but it's out of the question."

Nicole sank back in her seat and quietly finished her lunch.

"If you're dying to help out, Nicole, how about cleaning my room today?" Mollie asked hopefully. "I did help you clean yours."

"Mollie!" Mrs. Lewis eyed her warningly.

"Well, just if you're not busy," Mollie added hastily.

"Sorry, Mollie," Nicole said. "I'll tell you what. When it's your turn to pack for college, I'll be sure to help."

"Thanks a lot," Mollie replied sarcastically.

Nicole glanced at her parents. "I still have more to do upstairs. If lunch is over, may I be excused?"

Her parents nodded, and Nicole quickly left the table. She didn't really have anything pressing to do, she'd just felt the sudden need to be alone.

"Mollie and I will clean up, Mom," Cindy offered when Nicole had gone. "We don't mind," she added, ignoring Mollie's glare.

Mr. Lewis raised his eyebrows. "Maybe we should keep Nicole at home—she seems to set a good example for you two." He pushed his chair back and stood up. "A good example for me, too. I nearly forgot to go to the recycling center."

"All the papers to be recycled are on the counter stool," Mrs. Lewis told him. "Thanks for cleaning up, girls. I do appreciate it," she added as she headed out of the kitchen.

When both their parents had left, Mollie turned to Cindy. "Thanks a lot. I only had plans to hit the mall after lunch."

"Relax, shrimp. This won't take that long."

Sighing, Mollie cleared the table while Cindy measured soap into the dishwasher. Five minutes later, the kitchen was clean.

"Mollie—I have an idea," Cindy whispered.

"Not more chores around the house?"

Cindy grinned. "It's not that—let's throw a surprise party for Nicole."

"What?"

"Why not—Mom will let us, I'm sure." The memory of the near-disastrous food fight at one of their parties had faded from both girls' minds.

"I don't know.... I guess it's a good idea."

"We'll invite all Nicole's friends," Cindy went on. "But we have to make sure no one tells her. Just think of the look on her face when we all yell 'surprise!' "

Mollie's brain clicked into gear. "Their last memory, before they all go their separate ways," she mused dramatically. "I think I like it."

"Nicole will like it—that's what's important."

"You're right. She'll love it. It'll be a great send-off." Suddenly Mollie frowned. "Cindy, do you ever wonder what it will be like around here? Without Nicole, I mean. I never really thought about it before."

"You haven't? I have. It'll be kind of lonely, you know?"

Mollie nodded. "Yeah, I might really miss her a lot."

The sisters exchanged wistful glances.

"And Nicole will be having so much fun back East, she'll never even notice we're not there," Mollie pointed out. "Oh, well," she added with a sigh, "I guess that's life."

"Right, shrimp. But let's not worry about that. We have a menu to plan."

"An all-French menu," Mollie said, grinning.

"Right," Cindy agreed, fetching paper and pencil. "Mom will have to help, of course, but we can plan most of it ourselves."

Putting their heads together, they began listing all Nicole's favorite foods, and all the things best suited to parties: hors d'oeuvres, quiches, and to top it off, pastries and Nicole's favorite chocolate mousse. Their mouths were watering just thinking about it.

Suddenly Nicole burst into the kitchen. "Nicole! What are you doing here?" Mollie cried guiltily.

"What are you doing?" Nicole answered back. "What's that paper?" Springing toward their party notes, Nicole made as if to grab the pad away. Mollie yanked it off the table.

"It's ... nothing," she said, hiding the pad behind her back. "Just a, uh, shopping list—I told you not to leave this pad on the table, Cindy."

"Well, excuse me!" Cindy replied. "I didn't realize it was illegal."

"Just don't do it again," Mollie scolded. "Or I'll have to take it away."

Mollie and Cindy pretended to quarrel, hoping to distract Nicole, but they didn't have to worry. Nicole had already turned her back and was rummaging through the kitchen, lifting everything on the counters and even checking under pots and pans.

"Nicole," Cindy asked curiously, "what are you doing?"

"Eh, moi?" Nicole acted as if she'd forgotten her sisters were even there. "Oh, looking for my college kit. Has either of you seen it?"

"What kit?" Behind Nicole's back Mollie carefully tore the page of party plans from the pad, folded it, and tucked it safely in her back pocket.

"*Mon Dieu*, my freshman information kit from college," Nicole said in exasperation. "You know. You've seen it a thousand times. A blue-and-gray folder, with all my papers about orientation week."

"Oh, that!" Mollie said.

"You've only had your nose buried in it for weeks," Cindy put in.

"Yeah," Mollie added. "You hardly notice anything else."

Relieved that Nicole suspected nothing, Mollie giggled and Cindy rolled her eyes teasingly, enjoying their new secret.

From the corner of her eye, Nicole noticed. She felt a sharp pang of resentment. Already she was shut out. She suspected their "notes" had nothing to do with shopping lists, but she wasn't about to pry into her sisters' plan. The way they were acting, they could hardly wait for her to leave the room.

A wave of self-pity swept through Nicole. They probably wouldn't notice when she was gone. Just then, Mollie let out a peal of laughter.

"Mollie, this is important to me," Nicole snapped. She hadn't meant it to sound so nasty, but immediately Mollie looked offended.

"Take it easy, Nicole. Your kit will turn up somewhere."

"*Mais oui*, but I know I had it before. Let's see, I came down for lunch, and then I got Winston his dog food . . . I know, I threw it here, on the stool. But it's gone now."

Mollie's blue eyes widened. "Uh-oh—were there

some magazines and newspapers on the stool, too?"

Nicole shrugged. "*Je ne sais pas*. I guess so."

Mollie groaned, and Cindy suddenly looked worried.

"So," Nicole asked, "what's the problem?"

"So," Mollie said importantly, "all that stuff on the stool was for the recycling center. Dad just left with it."

Nicole paled. "*Mon Dieu*," she gasped. "Recycling ... my whole college kit? My orientation week schedule?" Her voice rose in a panic. "That was my dorm room assignment and the dining hall hours and my meal-ticket number!" She held a hand over her heart, which was pounding so hard, she was sure her sisters could hear it.

"What will I do?" She closed her eyes and swallowed hard. "Let me think.... I'll have to call the admissions office and get another kit sent out. *Non, non*—there's no time! Maybe they can send it overnight express?" She sank into a chair, her head in her hands.

"*Mon Dieu*," she said over and over. "*Quel désastre!* What am I going to do? I won't know where to go or when to go anywhere. I'll be lost!"

Nicole covered her face with her hands, trying to recover from this awful shock. When she finally looked up, Cindy was staring at her as though she'd lost her mind, with a strange smile on her face.

"Don't laugh at me," Nicole cried. "Can't you see how important this is? I—"

"Uh, Nicole," Cindy interrupted, "why don't I just get in the other car and go after them?"

Nicole looked at her blankly.

"After all," Cindy continued calmly, "those papers aren't going anywhere yet. I mean, they'll still be at the recycling center. I'll just drive over and get your kit back."

"Oh." Nicole flushed red. She hid her shaking hands behind her back, suddenly embarrassed and relieved at the same time.

"I mean, it's no big deal," Cindy added, getting up and searching through her pockets for the car keys.

"Yeah, Nicole," Mollie added, "why are you falling apart all of a sudden? You're supposed to be good in a crisis. I mean, you're the one who's always telling me not to be so dramatic."

"That's enough," Nicole said firmly. "I ... I wasn't falling apart. I just, oh, you wouldn't understand." Smoothing her rumpled shirt where she had absentmindedly twisted it in worry, Nicole got up. She had regained her self-control, but still, she avoided her sisters' eyes.

She didn't know what was wrong with her. Mollie was right—she was always the one in control. It was humiliating that Cindy had been cool and collected, while Nicole had nearly had a nervous breakdown. What a topsy-turvy day! First, Mollie had done her packing for her, and now Cindy had to rescue her information kit!

"*Eh, bien*," Nicole said, with more of her usual confidence, "I'll go there myself."

"Let me drive," Cindy insisted, still eager to use her fairly new driver's license at any opportunity.

"I'll come, too," Mollie said.

"*D'accord*, but hurry up, both of you," Nicole

said, still feeling flustered. "I've got a lot to do today."

"Yes, ma'am," Cindy said sarcastically.

"Boy, Nicole, don't take our heads off," Mollie added. "Cindy just saved your life. You didn't even think of the recycling center."

"I would have it if you two weren't fighting and carrying on," Nicole defended herself. "Besides, I've got more important things on my mind than your silly squabbles!"

Trying extra hard to maintain a pose of dignity, Nicole led her sisters to the garage. Behind her she heard Mollie and Cindy whispering. Nicole knew she had been unfair, but did they always have to talk about her behind her back? All the way to the recycling center they chattered away in the front seat, with Cindy keeping one eye on the road, while Nicole sat silently in the back. When they arrived at the recycling center, however, Cindy and Mollie were suddenly quiet, leaving Nicole to give an embarrassing explanation.

Well, that's just like them, Nicole thought. They just had to come with me, but when it comes down to it, they let me make a fool of myself. But she had her freshman information kit back, and that's what mattered most.

Chapter 3

"Cindy—mon Dieu! *Watch out for that car!*"
Nicole hid her eyes with her hands.

"No problem." Cindy jerked the wheel, pulling
the car into the middle lane.

Nicole's heart was beating hard. "Just get us to
the mall in one piece," she pleaded.

Cindy turned to face Nicole, sitting next to her
in the front seat. "I will," she assured her sister.
"Stop being so nervous."

"Turn around, *idiote*," Nicole shrieked, as a car
pulled in front of them, changing lanes. "Please
be more careful!"

"Nicole has a point, dear," Mrs. Lewis said from
the back. "You did take that entrance ramp rather
fast."

"Mother," Cindy groaned, "no back seat driving! You promised."

"I know, I know," Mrs. Lewis said hastily, "but
you haven't done much freeway driving yet."

21

"How could I? You never let me! Nicole always has the car, whether I need it or not."

"Watch the road," Nicole shouted as Cindy turned almost completely around to talk to her mother.

"Don't shout," Cindy said icily. "I can hear perfectly well."

"She's not a bad driver," Mollie popped up from the back seat.

"Thank you," Cindy responded. "And I'd be a better driver if *someone* wasn't so jumpy." She glared at Nicole.

"Don't look at me," Nicole said. "This trip wasn't my idea."

"Well, it wasn't mine, either," Cindy said, still offended. "But I had the crazy notion it would be fun."

"You just wanted to drive," Mollie pointed out. "Anyway, how much farther is it?"

"I thought no mall was too far for Mollie Lewis," Cindy retorted.

"Hey, I'm on your side," Mollie said indignantly. "I thought we'd have fun today, shopping all together. But all we've done so far is squabble."

"Mollie's right about that," their mother murmured.

Cindy bent over the wheel. "Well, don't blame me. I might point out that Nicole is the one who needs the warm coat for college—which is the whole reason we're shopping to begin with."

"*Mais oui*, and I do appreciate Mother squeezing in the time to go, but I don't know why we have to drive so far," Nicole commented. Anxiously she stared at the exit signs. She knew this trip was a mistake. The truth was, she didn't want to be here at all. Group shopping was not her favorite thing. Mollie would be eyeing all the boys, and Cindy wouldn't care about anything but sports equipment. But her mother had been so excited about all of them shopping together that she hadn't had the heart to say no.

Now Laura Lewis said, "Well, the shops near home didn't have anything right. Eastern winters can be awfully cold."

Mollie wrinkled her nose, pretending to shiver. "Ugh. Nicole, I still think you should look at sweater jackets."

"Mollie, I told you," Nicole said patiently, "they wouldn't be warm enough. *N'est-ce pas*, Mother?"

"*N'est* . . . I mean, that's right."

Mrs. Lewis laughed and Mollie and Cindy joined in—Nicole's constant use of French phrases got to all of them at times, but they usually answered in English!

Nicole tried to join in their laughter but failed. Trying not to be a spoilsport, she made her voice sound extra enthusiastic.

"My college kit says to make sure my clothing is warm enough," she told them all.

"That dumb kit again," Cindy grumbled. "If I knew you had the whole thing memorized, I wouldn't have worried so much about getting it back yesterday."

"I don't think I'd like the cold," their mother said hastily, trying to cut off another squabble.

"I'm with you," Mollie answered. "I was made for California sunshine."

"No," Cindy teased, "*I* was made for California

sunshine. You were made for indoor lights ... of a shopping mall." She laughed loudly, then winked in the rear view mirror. "Only kidding."

"Very funny," Mollie said dryly. "Then, why are you here, Miss American Beach Bum? You could be home, surfing," she pointed out.

"Togetherness."

"And you thought you might find something to impress Grant when he comes home from Hawaii?" Mollie added.

"I don't need to impress Grant," Cindy said smugly. "He likes me just the way I am."

Laura Lewis piped up. "Enough, girls, I know you're only teasing, but it is nearly Nicole's last day at home. Let's make it a pleasant one." Fondly Mrs. Lewis reached over the front seat to pat Nicole's shoulder.

"It won't be the same without my oldest at home."

"Mom, don't get all sentimental," Cindy said in mock terror.

Nicole smiled as if Cindy's joke were funny, but a stab of queer nervousness shot through her stomach. Like Mollie and Cindy, she was used to California. And she had heard that eastern students were different from Californians: where Californians were into health food and the great outdoors, easterners were into grades. And they were supposed to be fast talking and intense. How would she ever compete with students like that?

How am I ever going to make friends at Briarwood? she fretted. I probably have absolutely nothing in common with anyone there. What if they make fun of me, or ignore me completely? Nicole liked to think of herself as mature and somewhat sophisticated, but compared to eastern girls, she might seem like a country hick.

She could hardly bear to think about it, and at the same time, she was ashamed of herself for feeling so frightened, like a little kid.

"Nicole?"

She snapped to, suddenly alert. *"Oui?"*

"Where do you think we should park?"

Startled, Nicole looked around her; somehow, they had left the freeway. The entrance to the mall was straight ahead and she hadn't even noticed.

"Oh, uh, near the main store," she replied.

"Just what I said," Mollie grumbled. "Why doesn't anyone ever listen to me?"

The department store was crowded with back-to-school shoppers. Mothers dragged small children down the busy aisles, while packs of teens clogged the display areas. Nicole led the way, feeling oddly upset by the whole process. She was getting a headache from the heat and noise, and worse, no one else seemed to mind a bit. Her mother kept finding beautiful things to stop and examine, Mollie held back every time she spotted an especially cute boy, and Cindy was distracted by the racks of brightly colored sweat suits.

"Cheer up, Nicole," Mollie said breezily. "This isn't exactly torture."

"Maybe not for you," Nicole replied. "This place is a madhouse."

Mollie looked at her sister as though she'd

gone crazy. "But that's the fun of shopping. Take it from an expert," she added with a grin.

"Oh, never mind." Trying to act cheerful, Nicole headed toward the escalator. A store directory was posted next to it. "We came to buy a coat, *n'est-ce pas*? Well, the coats are upstairs. Let's go."

But no sooner had Nicole gotten halfway up the escalator than she heard her name being shouted. Then she saw that the others had gotten stuck behind a crowd of people. Waving frantically, they stood at the bottom of the escalator, shouting instructions.

"Nicole—meet us in junior coats," her mother yelled, as if Nicole wouldn't have thought of that herself!

"Did you hear me? Nicole!"

On the escalator, the two girls in front of Nicole turned around to stare.

At first Nicole pretended she had nothing to do with the screaming people at the bottom of the escalator, but then Mollie and Cindy joined in.

"Nicole? Did you hear?"

"Yes, yes, I heard," Nicole mouthed, waving hastily. Using sign language, she pointed in the direction of junior coats. Flushing with embarrassment, she ducked past the two girls and ran toward the coats department.

"Oh, no! Not more of them!" In front of her was another huge display of casual sweats—pants, pullovers, and cardigans—and a big, cheery sign:

WELCOME, SHOPPERS!
JUNIOR COATS HAVE BEEN MOVED

TO THE MAIN FLOOR
SORRY FOR THE INCONVENIENCE!

Nicole felt ready to scream.

"Oh, no," Mollie groaned, appearing beside her. "Downstairs, again?"

"What a shame." Mrs. Lewis straightened her shoulders. "Well, come on, girls—downstairs it is."

"Wait, Mom," Cindy grabbed her mother's arm. "Can't we just look at these first? I could really use a new pullover for school. Just a second, okay?"

"Maybe just for a second . . ."

"Ooh," Mollie squealed. "That clerk is adorable. Wait, Cindy—I'll come with you."

"Make it quick, girls," Mrs. Lewis said amiably while Nicole sighed angrily.

"*Mon Dieu*, Mother! Do you think I'm going to wait around for them all day?"

"Why, Nicole, what's wrong?"

"What's wrong?" Nicole glared at all of them. "I've been pushed and shoved and trampled, and we haven't even seen one coat yet! I will not wait for Cindy. Or Mollie, either. I'm fed up. I wish I had come on my own."

"Nicole!" Mrs. Lewis looked so hurt, Nicole softened her voice.

"Mother, I'm sorry, but this just isn't working."

"What do you want us to do?" Mollie demanded. "It isn't our fault the store's so crowded."

"I know, but you poke along. . . ."

"So what?" Mollie said. "We're not in a race or anything."

"I'll only be a minute anyway," Cindy added.

Nicole groaned. "You said that downstairs."

"Gee, it's not like I came along for your sake or anything," Cindy said sarcastically.

"She's right, Nicole. We planned this for you."

"I know, Mother. I'm sorry, but ..." Nicole felt tears welling up in her eyes. This was ridiculous! Taking a deep breath, she forced a smile. "Maybe I'd do better on my own."

"What do you mean?"

"It's not your fault, Mother," Nicole said hastily. "But everyone's pulling me in different directions."

"I'm not pulling anyone," Mollie declared.

"I don't see what you're so upset about," Cindy added.

Nicole appealed to her mother again. "Maybe I could run on ahead."

"But, Nicole," Mrs. Lewis protested, "this was supposed to be our day together. All of us."

"*Bien sûr*, but, maybe I could just meet you all later?" Nicole bit her lip. Her mother looked so disappointed!

"I know," Nicole burst out, "we could meet for lunch. I'll shop by myself for a while, and then, uh, we could meet someplace. How about that new restaurant by the mall entrance? It looked good."

"I don't know, Nicole...."

Nicole checked her watch. "Say, in an hour? No, an hour and a half. You don't mind, do you, Mother?"

"Well, if that's what you want," Mrs. Lewis said, giving Nicole a worried glance. "I thought we could all—"

"I know, but I just need to be alone." Unable to meet her mother's eyes, Nicole looked down.

Her mother sighed. "Okay, then." She opened her purse and pulled out a credit card. "Here, pay for the coat with this."

Nicole took the card. "Thanks, Mom," she said gratefully.

"What was the restaurant called? The Salad Bowl?" her mother asked.

"That's it." Trying to hide the relief she felt, Nicole backed away. "See you later then. Bye!" Waving, Nicole turned and nearly ran for the down escalator.

She felt terrible, deserting her mother that way. And her sisters, too. She didn't know what was wrong with her, but two more minutes of group shopping and she would have started screaming at everyone or else burst into tears. She just wasn't herself lately. But as she wandered aimlessly through the mall, Nicole felt her spirits rise. Maybe she did need to be alone. In a way, it was almost funny—her sisters acting so offended, when they hadn't done one bit of shopping for Nicole!

A store window caught her eye—that long blue coat was exactly what she had in mind! Nearly holding her breath, she ventured inside. The whole back wall was filled with nothing but warm winter coats. Nicole couldn't believe her good luck.

"That would look lovely on you," a saleswoman said as Nicole pulled a soft wool coat from the rack. The woman stood back, squinting. "Perfect color. For college?"

"Yes," Nicole said proudly. "In the East."

"I thought so." The saleswoman nodded knowingly. "We try to have warmer things for just that reason. We get a lot of girls shopping to go away to school. It can be hard to find a good winter coat around here."

"I know all about it," Nicole agreed. "They didn't have anything around Santa Barbara."

"Let me show you something else," the woman offered. She led Nicole to a circular rack stuffed with cotton coats in myriad colors.

"Down filled," the woman assured her. "Very popular with the college crowd. Simple design, isn't it? But it can be dressy as well as casual."

"I love it." Nicole admired the classic design. "A neutral color is more practical, isn't it?" She pulled a dove-gray coat from the rack.

The saleswoman smiled. "Try this too—for fun." She handed Nicole a hot-pink version. "I'll bring you several to try on."

"Some wool ones, too," Nicole said anxiously.

The saleswoman led her to a dressing room, and Nicole spent several minutes wrapping the different coats around her.

It was hard to choose. Finally, though, she settled on one of the down coats. This will be warmer than wool, she thought. The coat's clean lines looked well with her jeans, but just to make sure, the saleswoman brought Nicole a skirt to try on, and the coat looked wonderful with that, too.

"I'll take this one," Nicole said firmly, handing her choice to the woman. Nicole was pleased with her purchase, and she knew her mother would approve. The coat was very practical, but a little different, too, reversing from a lovely soft gray to a vivid bright blue. And Mollie would adore the clever snaps on the front.

"It's a lovely coat," the woman assured her. Nicole handed over her mother's credit card and the saleswoman wrapped the coat neatly and slid it into a huge shopping bag.

"I think so," Nicole agreed. Hoisting the bag, she felt positively elated. She had found the perfect coat, and in no time at all! She checked her watch—plenty of time to make it to the restaurant. Confidently she strode into the mall toward the nearest escalator. But she suddenly froze—this wasn't the way she had come. This didn't look at all familiar! People pushed up behind her and muttered apologies; Nicole backed out of their way.

How silly—how could she have gotten turned around? Striding in the opposite direction, she came to a dead-end wall and an elevator for handicapped only. This was completely wrong!

Face burning, she turned again. This was ridiculous—she had absolutely no idea where she was going!

"*Idiote*," she murmured to herself. "Stay calm, you're not a baby. Retrace your steps."

She turned right and then left, and came to the escalator again. Her head started spinning. This was ridiculous—she was too old to be lost! The only thing to do was sit down, take a deep breath and get her bearings. Relieved at this sensible plan, Nicole hurried to a group of benches surrounding a small rock garden in the center of the concourse. Surely she could figure out the right direction. Setting her bag carefully between her feet, she tried to concentrate. But a couple of girls had sat on the other side of her bench, behind her, and despite herself, Nicole ended up listening to their conversation instead.

"What dorm are you in?" the blond girl asked.

"Dorm? You're crazy! I got my apartment."

"Ginny! That's fantastic! Where?"

"In the Heights. And it is so cute."

"You're kidding! The Heights?"

"Uh-huh," Ginny said smugly. "Sandy and I have our own bedrooms and there's a fabulous living room and a deck and a fireplace."

Her friend groaned in envy. "A fireplace?"

"For sure—for romantic evenings."

"With Steve, right?"

"Maybe, if he plays his cards right."

They giggled together. Nicole sneaked a peek over her shoulder. They didn't look any older than she! But they sounded like seniors, at least.

"What's happening with you and Steve?" the blonde asked.

"We're on and off," Ginny replied. Then she laughed slyly. "But I took all independent studies this term, so I'll have lots of free time. Know what I mean?"

"Better save some time to study," her friend warned.

"No problem, I aced my exams. And papers don't faze me.'"

"Not even soc. or mod. lit.?"

"No problem. This year I'm majoring in party, party, party." They both laughed.

Nicole slumped on the bench, trying to be invisible. They sounded so sure of themselves, so full of plans—apartments and boys and "soshe" and "mod litt," whatever that was! On the other hand, Nicole had signed up for all the required freshman classes—not even one independent study. And to her, dorm living was the height of independence! An apartment was unthinkable. She didn't want to live all on her own. She was just a kid!

The gnawing feeling started in her stomach again. If only one of her friends was going to Briarwood College with her. Nicole bit her thumbnail. She had never felt more alone. Or more unsure of herself. To put it plainly, she was scared stiff. A tear dropped onto the back of her hand. Mortified, she grabbed a tissue from her purse and pretended to have a cold. Springing up from the bench, she ran blindly in the other direction. The coat store! She ran inside, her heart pounding.

"What's the matter dear? Did you forget something?"

The saleslady was staring at her.

"I, uh, I left my purse in the dressing room," she stammered.

The woman gave her a suspicious look. Her purse was slung over her shoulder, Nicole realized, flushing in embarrassment.

"Not my purse, *je sais* ... I mean ..." Humiliated, she backed out of the store.

"*Imbecile*," she cursed herself. "*Idiote*." Now she felt like a complete fool. Sure that everyone in the mall was staring, she coughed and dabbed at her eyes, still pretending to have a cold. Spotting a public restroom, she dashed inside, locking herself into a booth.

Now the tears poured out. Nicole could hardly believe herself—she never cried in public! She felt like a little girl on the first day of school, afraid to leave home without her mother.

Angrily she tore a fresh tissue from her purse to wipe her eyes. How could she act this way? She didn't understand herself.

"Mon Dieu!" She was half an hour late for lunch. Hastily she smoothed her hair and got out her eyeshadow. I'd better put myself back together and find that darned restaurant! she told herself.

Chapter 4

"**C**ome on, Mom," Mollie pleaded. "I'll die if we don't eat soon."

Mrs. Lewis glanced at her watch again and sighed. "I guess we may as well order. I can't imagine why Nicole is so late."

"She's probably admiring herself in some dressing room," Cindy said. "Trying to decide between a million coats."

"It's not like her to be so late." Mrs. Lewis scanned her menu. "How does seafood salad sound to you girls?"

"Not as good as if you made it," Molly said cheerfully, "but at this point, I'd eat seaweed and be happy."

Mrs. Lewis laughed. "Thanks for the compliment—I think."

They placed their orders, but Mrs. Lewis kept turning to scan the entrance to the restaurant. "Maybe she forgot the name of this place?"

"Nicole is a big girl, Mom," Cindy said, helping herself to some bread. "She knows what to do if she gets lost."

"I know you're right," their mother admitted, "but ... Nicole just hasn't been herself lately. Haven't you noticed?"

Mollie and Cindy exchanged glances. "That's putting it mildly," Mollie said.

"She's so touchy, I hate to talk to her," Cindy added.

"Yes, that's just what I mean." Mrs. Lewis frowned as she broke a bread stick in half and chewed it distractedly. "Oh, well. It's normal, I suppose. This is a big step in Nicole's life. I'm sure she doesn't mean to act this way."

Cindy shrugged. "I guess she can't wait to leave."

"Yeah, but she's a real pain," Mollie complained. "Acting like we're always in her way. Like everything is our fault."

"You're exaggerating," their mother said.

Mollie shook her head vigorously. "No, I'm not. Like yesterday, I was helping her pack—and she practically threw me out of the room. Without a word of thanks!"

"I know," Cindy agreed. "She never thanked me for getting her precious college kit back."

"She does have a lot on her mind."

"But so do I," Cindy declared.

Mollie agreed. "I happen to be very busy myself."

"Getting ready for school?" Mrs. Lewis nodded approval.

"No—I meant her surprise party. And I'm getting pretty fed up with that, too. I have half a mind not to bother."

"You're right about that, shrimp," Cindy cracked. "You do have half a mind."

Mollie rolled her eyes. "Can we get serious, please?" She turned to her mother. "I mean it, Mom. Why should we put ourselves out for Nicole? She barely notices I'm alive lately, except when she thinks I'm annoying her."

"I feel the same way," Cindy declared.

Just then the waitress appeared with their food. "Doesn't this look delicious?" Mrs. Lewis smiled enthusiastically.

"Don't change the subject," Cindy said.

"I just can't believe you're serious," her mother answered. "You wouldn't cancel the party?"

"We might," Mollie answered. "Why shouldn't we call it off? I bet Nicole wouldn't care. She can't wait to leave home, so why bother anyway?"

"Don't confuse things," Mrs. Lewis cautioned. "Nicole may be excited about going to college, but I'm sure she'd appreciate a going-away party. Especially one her sisters gave her."

"Forget it," Cindy said dismissively, her mouth full of lettuce. "She won't miss us."

"I'm sure she will. Nicole cares about both of you."

"Ha!" Mollie dug into her food.

"She might not know it herself," their mother said thoughtfully, "but Nicole will miss you. Even if she isn't acting that way right now."

"She's giving you a hard time, too," Mollie pointed out. "She didn't even want to go shopping with you." Mollie yelped as Cindy kicked her under the table.

"She didn't mean that the way it sounded,

Mom—Nicole loves to shop with you," Cindy said wryly.

Mrs. Lewis smiled. "Thank you, Cindy. But really, we all love Nicole, and she deserves a special send-off."

"Then, the party is on?"

"Absolutely," Mrs. Lewis said firmly. "The party is on."

"Well, I'll do it, but I won't enjoy it," Mollie grumbled.

"Too bad, shrimp—all that cooking will be a real drag," Cindy teased, then screeched as Mollie kicked *her* under the table.

"Cooking what?" Nicole, looking frazzled, dropped into the extra chair.

"Nicole! Where were you? I was getting worried," Mrs. Lewis greeted her.

"You started without me?" Nicole glanced at their half-eaten food.

"Sorry, honey," their mother apologized. "But you were very late."

"Yeah, Nicole," Mollie piped up, "I know you can't stand shopping with us, but did you have to avoid eating lunch with us, too?"

"It wasn't that at all!" Red-faced, Nicole protested. "I, uh, lost track of time, that's all."

"I told you," Mollie said. "Too busy to think about us." She tried to look stern, but her curiosity got the better of her. Eyeing Nicole's shopping bag, her fierce look softened. "What did you get?"

"Oh—just a coat."

"Wonderful!" Mrs. Lewis beamed as Mollie and Cindy demanded to see the new purchase.

"I don't want to get it dirty," Nicole murmured

as she pulled the coat from the shopping bag. "I might have to take it back."

"But why? It's a lovely color," her mother assured her.

Mollie oohed and aahed over the bright blue.

"And it reverses." Nicole demonstrated, turning back the lapel to show the soft gray cloth.

"I love the snaps," Mollie crooned. "It's a great coat."

"Yeah," Cindy chimed in, "even I like it."

"Do you really?" Nicole looked unconvinced.

"You did well," her mother insisted. "Then the trip was a success."

"Oui, mais . . ." Nicole hesitated.

"What is it, sweetheart? Not having second thoughts, are you?"

"Maybe," Nicole said haltingly. "I mean, it is a major purchase. I don't want to take the wrong thing."

Mollie rolled her eyes. "That's just like you, Nicole—worried about what everyone else will have. Be daring."

"That's not it," Nicole insisted. "It's just . . . college is so far away. If I made the wrong choice, I'll be stuck." At the sound of her own words, Nicole flushed. Was she talking about the coat, or was she really talking about college? *What am I getting myself into?* she thought. *I don't want to be stuck at Briarwood! What if I've made the wrong choice?*

"It's not too late."

"What?" Nicole stared at her mother. Had she read her mind?

But Mrs. Lewis smiled casually. "It's not too

late to take the coat back. Try it on for us after lunch, and if you've really changed your mind, we'll return it."

"Oh." Nicole gulped. For a moment, she had thought her mother had meant that it wasn't too late for her to change her mind about Briarwood! To cover her confusion, Nicole became brisk and efficient, tucking the coat neatly into the shopping bag. "I'll try it on after we're done eating."

"Fine. No use having second thoughts all the way home."

"Mother . . ." Nicole hesitated. "You will tell the truth? If you don't like it, I could get something else."

"I'm sure it will be fine. I trust your judgment, Nicole."

Nicole nodded. The waitress approached to take her order. "Oh, I'll have the Salade de Provence," Nicole said, her pronunciation flawless, as usual.

"That's more like it," Mollie remarked. "Now you sound like the Nicole Lewis we all know. For a minute there, I wasn't sure it was you."

"No such luck, Mollie!" Nicole replied. "I'm afraid you're stuck with me—at least for the rest of the week, anyway."

Nicole had meant her remark to sound like lighthearted banter, but inside her heart was heavy.

Chapter 5

Sunlight poured through the hall window—it was a perfect day for a barbecue! Her spirits high on this glorious summer Tuesday, Nicole bounded down the stairs. "I'm going," she called over her shoulder. "Be back sometime tonight!"

"Nicole—wait!" Cindy ran through the kitchen to the garage door. "I was supposed to have the car today!"

"But Bitsy's party—I'll be gone all day." Nicole shook her head in annoyance. "Sorry, Cindy. Another time."

"No, wait," Cindy pleaded. "Can't you get a ride? I need the car. A bunch of us are planning to try a new surfing beach today, and it's too far to bike. In fact, I'm supposed to pick up Duffy in half an hour."

"Surfing! Is that all you think about?" Impatiently Nicole tapped her foot. "This is the party of the year. It's the final bash before everyone goes to college. I might never see some of these people again."

"Nicole, please? I need the car."

"What if the party is over late? How am I supposed to get home?"

"You can get a ride from someone. I'll take you to Bitsy's. Pretty please, Nicole?"

Exasperated, Nicole gave in. "Okay, okay," she said finally. "I suppose I'll find a ride home."

Nicole hated to admit that she didn't really *need* the car— only it would be nice if she could offer someone else a ride home instead of begging for one herself. She would have felt more independent. But, truthfully, a little inconvenience couldn't stop her from enjoying the party. She was really looking forward to seeing Bitsy and the whole crowd from school. Everyone had been so busy lately getting ready for college that she hadn't seen much of her friends at all.

"Thanks, Nicole. I really mean it." Cindy slid into the passenger seat of the car. "I won't even ask if I can drive."

Nicole raised an eyebrow and laughed good-naturedly. "That's a change."

Cindy stared at her. "Now you're in a good mood?"

"I'm really looking forward to this party. It's my only chance to see everyone before school."

"Really?" Cindy bit her lip—Nicole would be shocked to know that Bitsy wasn't the only one planning farewell parties. Nicole's party would be a total surprise. Enjoying her secret, Cindy pretended to be confused. "I don't know—maybe Bitsy's making too much of a fuss about it."

"What fuss?"

"You know," Cindy answered innocently, "a big barbecue for all those kids. Too complicated."

Nicole's eyebrows rose in a very superior manner. "You just don't understand. Wait until you have to leave your oldest friends behind."

"Big deal," Cindy said, smiling to herself. "I'd be too excited about the future to worry about the past."

"You're wrong," Nicole stated flatly. "You'd care. I can't believe you're *that* insensitive, Cindy."

"I'm not insensitive," Cindy declared. "Just practical. You should worry about making new friends. Your old friends will always be around, no need to worry about that." Grinning, she turned teasing eyes to her older sister and was surprised that Nicole's happy smile had vanished.

"Well, I want to make the most of the time I've got left with my old friends," Nicole said seriously.

"Hey, Nicole, lighten up. I was kidding," Cindy assured her. "Of course, I'd miss my old friends if I were going away. Anybody would be crazy not to."

"But, making new friends ..." Nicole hesitated. "Do you think it's harder in college?"

Cindy shrugged. "No, probably not. I don't know."

Nicole gave her a halfhearted smile. "Okay. Forget it."

But Cindy's words had startled her. Secretly, Nicole agreed—she should be looking forward to the future. She had been, until the last few days. She shook off her sudden anxiety.

"You're right, Cindy," she burst out. "I am excited about the future. Very excited."

Cindy gave her a strange look. "You don't have to convince me. I believe you."

Nicole laughed. "One thing—at least, at college I won't have to play chauffeur anymore."

At Bitsy's, Nicole got out and Cindy slid into the driver's seat. "Listen," Cindy suddenly said, "if you get stuck for a ride, call home. I'll try to get back early."

"*Merci*—but it's okay. I'm sure I'll get a ride.

Bitsy's backyard had been transformed. Crepe paper streamers were strung everywhere, and brightly colored balloons reached up for the sky. Wherever Nicole looked, decorations fluttered in the breeze. Picnic tables had been set up near the house, and they were already covered with food— chips and dips and assorted platters of tiny egg rolls, miniature pita sandwiches and vegetable sushi. Meanwhile, smoke billowed around the built-in barbeque, where Bitsy and some of the guys from their class were just starting the coals.

For the first few minutes Nicole was busy just saying hello to all her friends. Everyone was there—her closest friends, of course, but also some kids from school that Nicole had only known slightly. Bitsy had really pulled out the stops. There was enough food to feed an army, and Bitsy had invited a small army to demolish it!

"Nicole!" Kelly Wenniger threw her arms around Nicole's shoulders. "I'm going to miss you!"

"Kelly—you're crying." Nicole rummaged through her pockets for a clean tissue.

"I can't help it." Kelly gulped. "I get so senti- mental. Saying goodbye ... I almost wish senior year had never happened. Then we would still all be together."

Wistfully Nicole hugged her friend. "I know exactly what you mean." She felt tears well up in her own eyes.

"Hey—not at my party!" Bitsy was suddenly at Nicole's side, brandishing a pair of barbecue tongs. "No tears—that's an order." Acting fierce, Bitsy waved the tongs at Nicole.

"Sorry, Bitsy," Kelly cut in, "it's my fault. I didn't mean to start, but . . ."

Bitsy pretended to scowl at Kelly. "Shape up," she ordered. "Think fun, Kelly—fun."

"But it's so awful." Kelly's smile wavered and she wailed helplessly, looking for a dry shoulder to cry on.

As Kelly left, Bitsy turned to Nicole and sighed. "Let's save the crying for later."

Nicole smiled. "Sorry, I couldn't help it. Kelly is right—I will miss everyone so much!"

"Well, miss them tomorrow," Bitsy said.

Realizing that her friend was serious about not wanting to ruin the party mood, Nicole flashed her brightest smile. "No problem. I'm recovered already—see?"

"That's a relief." Bitsy nodded and waved at some new guests. "Grab some food," she yelled, then turned back to Nicole. "You know, I'm surprised at you. You're not the teary type."

"*C'est vrai,*" Nicole agreed. "I guess my family is right—I haven't been myself lately."

"Is anything wrong?" Bitsy immediately looked concerned.

Nicole said jokingly, "Not really. College nerves."

"Me, too," Bitsy confessed. "My mom is driving me crazy. She's convinced I have nothing to wear. And my dad . . ."

"Oh, I didn't mean my family. They're okay. They're looking forward to it." Nicole grinned. "Mollie is ecstatic about getting my old clothes, and Cindy can't wait to have the car to herself."

"I know." Bitsy nodded. "My folks keep dropping hints about second honeymoons and finally being alone together. It's kind of insulting." But Bitsy's broad smile made it clear she didn't really mind. She noticed someone about to drink from a giant bottle of Coke. "Hey, Norris," she cried, "there are paper cups here. Please?" Bitsy shook her head indulgently. "Can you believe it? I'm actually going to miss a slob like Norris?" She grinned. "But it is sad, friends breaking up and all," she added to Nicole.

"Yes, and going away from home, for real. I've been away for trips and vacations, but this isn't the same thing." Nicole frowned.

"It sure isn't," Bitsy agreed. But she was looking over Nicole's shoulder. "No one's touched the guacamole! Could you pass it around, Nicole?"

"Sure. Anything else?"

Bitsy gave her a quick hug. "Just play assistant hostess while I get the barbecue going, will you?"

Nicole flashed her brightest smile. "Count on me."

"I will. Thanks." With a backward wave Bitsy hurried toward the barbecue pit, shouting orders not to bury the coals.

Nicole took the biggest tray of chips and guacamole dip and began to circulate through the crowd.

"Is that Bitsy's famous guacamole?" Cara Grossman said, eyeing the tray.

"Take a paper plate," Nicole suggested. "You can fill it up."

"And you won't have to stand here while I pig out." Cara grinned. "Good idea." Cara helped herself. "Nicole, I never congratulated you."

"For what?"

"Getting into Briarwood."

"Oh, thanks."

"It's a great school," Cara told her. "I've a cousin who went there. He said it's small enough to keep classes down but big enough to attract some top professors."

"He really liked it?" Nicole moved closer. She had always like Cara a lot, but somehow they had never spent much time together.

"Loved it. I almost envy you going there."

Nicole hesitated. "Almost?"

Cara grinned. "Don't get me wrong—Briarwood is a terrific place. I just meant, I could never get in there. Besides, I'm not sure I want to go to school. Junior college is more my speed."

"I don't know about that," Nicole protested.

Cara shrugged. "I figure, in two years I can transfer somewhere else if I want to."

"You'll want to." Sean Elliot leaned over Cara's shoulder to grab some chips and dip.

Nicole set the heavy tray on a table and turned back to Cara. "You really think a two-year college is right for you?"

"Absolutely. Besides, it's close to home. If you

weren't so set on Briarwood, I might try to talk you out of it," Cara said. "I'd love to have another friendly face around."

Sean grimaced at her. "Isn't mine enough for you?"

Cara put her hand against Sean's face and pretended to push him away. "Your face is another story."

Nicole smiled. She only knew Sean slightly. He was heavily into sports and had been in a different crowd from hers at Vista High. But she knew he and Cara were good friends. She turned to him. "Are you going to junior college too?"

"No way," Cara answered for him. "Sean's too smart."

Sean acted offended. "I guess Nicole thinks only eastern guys are smart."

"That's not what I meant at all," Nicole protested. She wasn't sure if Sean was serious or teasing.

"California guys are hip," he declared. "And everyone knows easterners are wimps."

Nicole hesitated, then tossed her head defiantly. "I don't know about that. What about Ivy League football?"

Sean winced. "Yeah, okay—but can they surf?"

With relief Nicole realized he was teasing. "Maybe not," she said breezily, "but then, they don't have to."

"Traitor!" Sean's blue eyes sparkled. "Another California girl gone eastern," he complained to Cara. "You'll see, she'll forget all about us hometown guys."

"I haven't left yet," Nicole pointed out.

"Well, our loss is their gain," Sean quipped.

Nicole didn't know what to say. Was that a compliment, or a joke? The sun was shining in her eyes and she raised a hand to shade them as she inspected Sean's face. His dark hair gleamed in the sunlight, curly and tousled. She had to admit he was as good-looking as most girls said he was, but his manner was unsettling—how was she supposed to know if he was teasing or serious?

"So, I guess you are staying in California to go to college?" she asked carefully.

"Good old University of California at Santa Barbara." He gave a small salute. "It's a dirty job, but someone has to do it. Besides, I have to keep an eye on Cara."

Cara grimaced. "As if I had anything to do with it. He got a great scholarship, " she told Nicole. "And it's a good thing we're only friends," she added, "because as soon as those freshman girls get a look at him, that's the last I'll see of Sean Elliot."

"Not a chance," Sean swore. "I'll schedule a visit after my first fifty dates."

Behind them someone complained loudly that the guacamole had disappeared.

"I'd better go." Nicole moved toward the tray.

"Let me." Cara grabbed the tray first.

"I'll do it," Nicole protested, "I promised Bitsy."

"I don't mind," Cara insisted. "Let me play hostess."

"Yeah, you can use the practice," Sean cracked.

Making a face at him, Cara moved away.

Nicole stood there awkwardly. "Cara is really

nice," she finally said. "I always wished I knew her better."

Sean examined her. "Really? You and Cara don't seem to have much in common."

"What do you mean by that?"

Sean shrugged, grinning at her in a disarming way. "Don't get insulted. I just meant, we kid around a lot. I always thought of you as the serious type."

"I didn't know you thought of me at all," Nicole replied smoothly.

Sean raised his eyebrows. "Every guy in the class thought about Nicole Lewis. I just thought you were, you know, all work and no play."

Nicole bristled, taken aback. But then she flashed a smile. "But you don't know me very well."

"Maybe I made a mistake. Sorry."

Nicole grinned. She felt she'd earned a point. "I guess I forgive you."

"Thanks. You know," he said pleasantly, "Cara's right—it is too bad so many of our friends are going away. Did you apply to any local schools?"

"Not really," Nicole admitted. "Briarwood was the only place I really wanted to go."

Sean frowned. "It's a pretty tough school, isn't it?"

Nicole felt uncomfortable. Sean would say she was too serious again. "Well, it has the classes I wanted."

"Oh, yeah? Like what?"

"French literature, mostly." She paused. "I guess UCSB must have some pretty good sports teams—as well as academics, I mean."

To her surprise, Sean shook his head thoughtfully. "Actually, going to UCSB doesn't have much to do with sports or academics."

"Then, why?"

"Are you really interested?"

"Yes, I am. Really." Nicole sat on a picnic bench, and Sean sat next to her.

"Well ..." He took a deep breath. "To be honest, I think we're under enough pressure. Freshman year is tough; everyone says so. I figure, why make it harder by going away?"

"But what difference would that make, really?"

Sean looked at her closely. "To me—a lot of difference. You heard Cara just say that I have a scholarship. Well, I've got to keep my grades up. In a new place, I'd have to learn my way around, and I'd want to see the sights."

"Everyone would do that," Nicole agreed.

"Right. But I can't afford to waste the time. By staying here I'm already half-adjusted. I already know my way around, so I only have to worry about classes."

"That makes some sense," Nicole admitted. "Do you remember Lisa Colville? She was a year ahead of us at Vista."

Sean nodded.

"Well, I ran into her at Taco Rio a few weeks ago. She told awful stories about freshman year," Nicole said. "Lots of kids have trouble adjusting. They go from being well known in a small high school to being completely unknown in a big college. It really throws some people."

"I've heard that, too." Sean nodded.

"Lisa really hated the social pressures. She said there was a party every night, and then sorority rushing, and then football games and mixers. She was neglecting classes. Finally, to keep from flunking out, she ended up staying in all the time to study."

"That's no good, either," Sean said. "I mean, everyone has to party a little. Otherwise, you get crazy. It's not good for you."

"I'm sure you could work out a compromise," Nicole suggested.

"How? Suppose it's a choice between studying or making new friends? Which would you do?"

"But that's always hard," Nicole protested. "You make those choices in high school, too."

"High school isn't college," Sean pointed out. "College is hard. And you shouldn't make it any harder."

Nicole searched Sean's face for signs of teasing, but he was completely serious now. She found herself half agreeing with him.

"Actually," she said slowly, "I have thought about that. In fact, I've been a little worried about it lately," she admitted. "Wondering if going away was the right choice. I know what you mean, about pressure. I'm already worried about classes, and suddenly I'm nervous about making new friends."

"That's it," Sean cried excitedly. "That's exactly how I felt. Just thinking about it made me nervous." He grinned. "Though I know that's hard to believe."

Nicole grinned back. She was getting to know when Sean was kidding and when he wasn't. She was suddenly sorry she had always dismissed Sean so lightly before. Uncomfortably she won-

dered if she *had* been too serious in high school—
too serious to get to know a bright, attractive boy
like Sean. Sean liked to party, but he cared about
grades, too. And there was nothing wrong with
teasing and joking as long as he knew when it
was time to be serious.

Suddenly Bitsy grabbed Nicole's arm, pulling
her off the picnic bench.

"Do something! This party is dying."

Nicole looked around. The yard was packed.
"What's wrong?" she asked.

"Get these people dancing," Bitsy cried. "They
can't just stand here." She propelled Nicole across
the lawn. "Change the music—do something."

"I'll try." A little annoyed that Bitsy had taken
her away from Sean, Nicole nevertheless went
into the house and sorted through the stacks of
cassette tapes that Bitsy had lined up. She put on
a popular tape, and when she glanced up, things
were really jumping.

She caught sight of Sean dancing wildly with
Cara. She was inching toward them when Mike
Evans looped an arm around her waist and swung
her around. Before she knew it, Nicole was swept
up into the music. Normally she was a good dancer
but very controlled. Today, however, she let herself go. After all, it was the end of an era for her,
and she wanted to have the best time possible
before the good times became only memories.

Chapter 6

*A*t a break in the music Kelly bounded over, her address book flapping open. "Nicole—everyone's exchanging college addresses. I don't have yours!"

Nicole took the pen Kelly offered and scribbled the address for Briarwood College.

"Nicole—sign my book, too." Diana Meyers and Yvette Rivers came up with their address books, and while Nicole wrote down her college address two more times, Lisa and Yvette filled in Nicole's book with their new addresses.

"I'm getting writer's cramp," Nicole joked.

"Well, don't worry," Lisa told her. "We probably won't have time to write all these letters anyway."

"Yeah," Yvette agreed. "Don't count on me. I'm better with a telephone."

"Your phone bill will be astronomical." Lisa nodded. "Keeping in touch long distance."

"You're right." Nicole thought of the monthly allowance she and her parents had agreed to. "I can't even afford to call home much. I think I'd better brush up on my letter writing."

Lisa sighed. "If it comes down to phone calls or new clothes, I don't know what will happen. Maybe I'll buy a new pen and some stationery." Lisa turned as Sean approached the group. "Sean—write your address."

"You already know it," Sean said. "I'll be at home."

"You're not in a dorm?" Lisa seemed surprised.

Sean shook his head. "Nope. But I have got a sort of traveling dorm." He winked.

"What's that?" Nicole asked.

"My new car. It was either live in the dorm and no car, or live at home and get new wheels."

"Not a bad deal," Yvette said. "You can still hang out at school all you want."

"Right." Sean grinned. "And drive home for decent meals and fresh clothes. That's my plan."

"You make it sound so good," Nicole remarked.

"I think it is." Sean eyed her address book. "That thing is bursting at the seams. Think you could squeeze in one more name?"

"Sure," Nicole answered, pleased that Sean had asked. It didn't take long for Sean to write down his address, but just as he finished, someone else called him away.

"He's really nice, you know," she commented to Diana and Yvette. "I never really knew him that well."

"No kidding?" Diana said in surprise.

"Actually, today is the first time we ever really talked," Nicole admitted.

"Now you know what you've been missing," Yvette remarked with a grin. "I thought everyone knew Sean. Where have you been all this time?"

"Busy, I guess." Nicole looked from Diana to Yvette. She was beginning to wonder if Sean was right about her—had she been too busy studying? Had she missed out on meeting great people? It must be true—otherwise, she couldn't have missed knowing Sean.

Just then Bitsy called, "Food's on!" There was a mad scamper toward the barbecue. For the next hour or so, Nicole was busy helping Bitsy serve chicken and burgers and even seafood shish kebab fresh off the grill, and making sure everyone had enough to eat.

In between her duties as assistant hostess she made the rounds. Suddenly there seemed to be so much to say to all her friends. She was amazed when the first few people started to say farewells. The party had barely started! But, in fact, the afternoon had fled. In no time at all it seemed the food was gone and most of the crowd had said good-byes and drifted away.

Sean tapped her elbow. "Still here?"

"I'm still helping," she explained. "Bitsy asked me to clean up some of this disaster." They both looked around—the clipped lawn was almost invisible under a layer of torn streamers and the paper plates and napkins that had been blown around in the strong breeze.

"I'll help." Sean followed Nicole around the yard with a huge trash bag as she collected debris and dumped it into the bag. They fell into a comfortable silence as they worked.

"Look—we're the last ones here," Sean remarked when the bag was nearly full.

"Are we?" Nicole looked up and gazed around in surprise. "I guess I don't want to leave. It will mean summer's really over."

"I know. But you'll be home soon, won't you?" Sean asked. "Thanksgiving vacation is not too far away."

"I hope so, but it's a pretty expensive trip," Nicole admitted. "I might have to wait for Christmas break instead."

"That's a long time. Won't you get homesick?"

"I'll be too busy." Nicole hoped she sounded more confident than she felt.

"Hey, you two." Bitsy bounded over and grabbed each of them in a big hug. "You're terrific. Thanks so much for helping."

"The party was great," Nicole told her. "I hated to see everyone leave."

"I know." Bitsy's eyes looked suspiciously red. "It's pretty sad, I guess."

The two girls looked at each other and Nicole felt her eyes mist over.

"None of that sentimental stuff," Sean declared. "Come on, look on the bright side. Think of all the new gossip you'll have for each other."

"I guess." Bitsy sniffed and dabbed quickly at her eyes. "This is really it."

Nicole forced a smile. "In four days I'll be gone."

"Oh, Nicole!" Bitsy flung herself at her best friend, and they hugged as if they'd never see each other again.

"You'd better come home for Thanksgiving," Sean told Nicole. "Bitsy won't make it otherwise."

Bitsy sniffed again. "He's right," she said mournfully.

"I'll call you every day before I leave," Nicole promised.

"You'd better," Bitsy told her. She hugged Nicole again. "I wish you could stay for dinner," Bitsy said, "but we're going out with my aunt and uncle. In fact, I'd better run and change."

Nicole frowned. "Oh—I thought you'd give me a ride home."

"I can give you a ride," Sean offered.

"That would be great," Bitsy said. "You don't mind, Nicole?"

"No, that's fine. You go get ready. I'll go with Sean."

"Great," Sean exclaimed "I get to show off my new car."

Bitsy gave Nicole one last hug. "Call me later, okay?"

"Okay."

It was hard to say good-bye to Bitsy, even if it wasn't their final farewell. Nicole turned to wave at least three times.

Sean's new car rode so smoothly, Nicole hardly noticed the bumps and dips in the twisty road. It was pleasant to lean back and enjoy the drive home.

"By the way," Sean remarked, "you're just missing UCSB's French culture program. They have it every fall. Did you know that?"

"No, not really. I mean, Mrs. Preston mentioned it in French class, but ..."

"I know—you were going East, so you didn't pay attention," Sean answered for her. "Too bad. They have French music and a film festival, and even cooking classes and language workshops."

"I didn't know that."

"Sure, it's in the catalog. You have seen the catalog, haven't you?"

"Well, no," Nicole admitted.

Sean shook his head as if he was very disappointed in her. "I see. You made up your mind without checking it out. Just because it's close to home doesn't make it bad."

"I know that," Nicole defended herself. "I just didn't ..." She stopped. Sean was right—she hadn't checked into UCSB because she'd already made up her mind to go to Briarwood.

Sean laughed at her expression. "It's not a crime. Hey, I have the catalog at home. I could lend it to you."

"That's nice of you, Sean," Nicole said, "but my plans are all fixed. I leave this Saturday."

"Can't hurt to look. We can swing by my place and pick it up right now. What do you say?"

Nicole hesitated. She wasn't about to change her college plans, but Sean's offer was so friendly, she hated to refuse.

"Well, all right."

Sean said earnestly, "Who knows? I might get lucky and convince you to stay here." He gave her a piercing look, and Nicole's heart fluttered strangely. "Like I said," he added, "it can't hurt to look."

"No," Nicole echoed, "it can't hurt."

Nicole bit her lip. Since splitting up with her boyfriend, Mark, nearly a year ago, she had really missed being part of a couple. And Sean was so cute! It was only a daydream, but if she did somehow go to UCSB instead, not only would she be near her old friends but perhaps she and Sean would get together.

It was a very attractive idea. The truth was, she hadn't been so intrigued with a boy in a long time—not since she had first gotten together with Mark. But it made no sense. Her college plans were definite. She couldn't change them now. Anyway, she didn't want to! It made no sense to dream about Sean when she was about to leave town.

Nevertheless, she stole a glance at his profile. She liked the way his lips curved in an easy smile, and she loved the way his curly hair was caught by the breeze blowing in through the open window. And his eyes were so full of laughter. She was even beginning to enjoy his constant joking.

But it's stupid, she told herself firmly. She was leaving town! If only she weren't. She frowned at herself. Why did this have to happen now? It didn't make any sense at all.

Chapter 7

The alarm clock shrieked. Mollie groaned and reached out blindly for the off-button before the alarm woke everyone in the house. Minutes later she headed down the stairs.

"Hurry," Cindy called from the kitchen. "We have to get out before Nicole gets up."

Mollie stretched and yawned. "I know this is a secret, but do we really have to go so early?"

Cindy nodded grimly. "You know how it is lately—anything Nicole wants, she gets—and if she wants the car, we don't stand a chance."

"So where do we get these decorations?" Mollie grabbed the cereal and poured herself such a huge bowl that she had to put half of it back in the box. It was messy work and Cindy stared at her impatiently.

"Can't you just grab some fruit?"

Mollie gave up, tipping the rest of the cereal back into the box. "Oh, all right. I'm ready, then."

"Good. Here, Mollie, you hold on to Mom's credit card until we need it," Cindy said, giving her sister the precious card. "Don't lose it."

Mollie took the card gladly. It wasn't often she was allowed to use it, but just holding it gave her a thrill.

Grabbing Mollie's elbow, Cindy pulled her sister out to the garage. "I love having the car."

"No kidding," Mollie muttered sarcastically, though, in fact, she got a kick of her own when she went out driving alone with Cindy. It made her feel so grown up. She couldn't wait to get her own license.

"The party store is over on Melrose," Cindy told her, squinting at the street signs. "I saw it the other day—there it is." Carefully Cindy pulled the car into a parking space. With a smile of satisfaction she put a coin in the meter and led Mollie through the front door.

"What are we getting anyway?" Mollie picked up a package of fancy paper doilies. "This stuff? Or this?" Doubtfully she frowned at a display of paper cups and plates decorated with cartoon characters.

"That's for kids," Cindy said firmly. "We want something bright but sophisticated."

"We do?" Mollie glanced around the huge store. "Then I think we need help."

"Somebody call me?" A lean boy with light brown hair and a smattering of freckles stepped toward them. He wore a red work smock with "Party Time!" embroidered above the pocket, and a name tag in the shape of a balloon that said his name was Richie.

"You must work here," Mollie said, a dazzling smile suddenly appearing on her face.

"Sure do. Can I help you?"

"I don't know where to begin," Mollie said helplessly.

"Oh, no," Cindy groaned. "Here we go again."

Mollie ignored her. "We need something very, very special."

"Special decorations for a special girl." Richie grinned, and Mollie felt her heartbeat quicken.

"I'm going to check out the centerpieces," Cindy told them. "Call if you need me."

Mollie nodded absentmindedly as Cindy headed for a display set up against the back wall of the store.

"So what do you need?" Richie asked Mollie.

"Oh! Well, it's, uh, for a going-away party." His green eyes were so gorgeous that Mollie almost forgot why she was there.

"Um-hm. You'll want banners and stuff like that," Richie suggested, leading her to another aisle. "How about this?" He held up a large banner with cut-out letters that said BON VOYAGE.

"Oh, no, not that kind of going-away party. It's for my sister—she's leaving for college."

"I see." Richie nodded. "So you want streamers and balloons."

"Not really." Quickly Mollie explained that they were giving Nicole a sit-down dinner. "She's really into cooking."

"Then you want plates, cups, dessert bowls, matching forks and knives, a tablecloth, napkins, and cocktail napkins." Richie pulled open a deep drawer. "How about these?"

He held up a paper plate with a bright design.

"I see—it says 'good-bye' in all different languages." Mollie nodded.

"Well, not really 'good-bye,'" Richie told her. "See, like it says '*auf Wiedersehen*' and '*au revoir*' —they really mean 'till we meet again.'"

"That's perfect," Mollie cried. "My sister is crazy about anything French!"

"Great. How many people?" Richie began piling the party goods on the floor.

"Well, I'm not exactly sure yet," Mollie admitted.

"Get twelve of everything," Richie suggested. "You can always use some extras."

"Good idea. I mean, this rich food could soak right through the plates anyway."

As Richie began to write up the order, Mollie described the lavish dinner that she and Cindy had planned.

"Sounds delicious," Richie commented.

"Do you like French food?"

"Who doesn't?"

"How about coq au vin and chocolate mousse and éclairs?"

"Ooh." Richie rubbed his stomach, looking suddenly famished. "All that?"

"It's simpler than it sounds," Mollie assured him.

"Not for me. I can't boil eggs."

"Oh, it's not so hard, if you have the right recipe," Mollie bragged.

Richie looked impressed. "You must be a great chef."

"Well," Mollie agreed modestly, "some of us just have the touch."

Richie picked up the stack of party goods and carried them toward the cash register. As she followed Richie, Mollie admired the curve of his strong shoulders. Imagine meeting such a cute boy in this store! If she'd had any idea this could happen, she would have worn her leggings and bright yellow top instead of her khaki shorts and T-shirt that made her skin look too pale.

Richie smiled at her. "How are you paying, by the way?"

Mollie flushed. "Oh! Credit card."

She handed him the card as if it were gold instead of plastic. A minute later he passed her the charge slip, and she dutifully wrote her name, address and phone number on the bottom. At last Richie gave her a huge shopping bag stuffed with the party supplies.

"Wow," she exclaimed in surprise. "This is heavy."

"Well, we could deliver," Richie told her, "if it's too much for you."

"Oh, no, it's not too much for me," Mollie declared. "Honest."

"But we don't mind delivery. Honest," Richie said with a grin. "I'll even deliver it myself if you give me a taste of the chocolate mousse."

Mollie eyed him flirtatiously. "Are you hinting for a party invitation?"

Richie laughed. "I'd do anything for chocolate mousse."

Mollie pointed to the charge slip. "You know my address," she told him. "Five-thirty on Friday."

"Sounds good."

Cindy came up to the register. "Look, Mollie,

I've got these dried flowers for a centerpiece," she said, holding up a straw basket filled with dried flowers in reds and yellows. "And this guest book."

"What's the guest book for?"

"You know—so everyone can sign in and write a message to Nicole."

"Like an autograph book?" Mollie asked.

"Sort of. They have guest books at weddings and things." Cindy placed the basket and the book on the counter. "We'll take these," she said to Richie.

"Cindy," Mollie said uncomfortably, "I already got everything."

"Excuse me," Richie interrupted, "more customers."

"Oh—well, thanks for your help," Mollie said.

"*Au revoir.*" Richie gave Mollie a brief salute and a special smile and went off to wait on some shoppers in the back to the store. Mollie stared after him, her eyes dreamy. "*Au revoir*" means "till we meet again!" she thought. Then he *would* come to the party!

"What do you mean, you got everything?"

"Exactly what I said. Everything."

Cindy eyed the shopping bag suspiciously. "Details, please."

"You know—plates, cups, napkins, and a tablecloth," Mollie recited. "And they all say 'farewell' in different languages and . . ."

"Hold it!" Cindy looked aghast. "Who said anything about paper plates and tablecloths?"

"What did we come here for?"

"For a centerpiece and maybe some nice party favors or something," Cindy answered.

"That's all?" Mollie hoisted the shopping bag. "But I got all this stuff."

"I don't believe it!" Cindy's mouth dropped open as she peeked in the shopping bag. "This is supposed to be an elegant, grown-up dinner party, with Mom's best linen tablecloth and napkins. A formal dinner, with crystal and silverware and candles . . ."

"Well, nobody told me," Mollie cried. "How was I supposed to know?"

"You were standing right there," Cindy fumed. "We discussed everything with Mom."

"I don't know what you're talking about," Mollie insisted. "I never heard any of it."

"Your mind was probably in outer space, as usual," Cindy grumbled. "Great. Just great. Real typical, shrimp."

"Well, what am I supposed to do?" Mollie felt sick to her stomach. "I just charged all this stuff."

"Return it."

"I can't!" Mollie turned bright red. "What would I say?"

"We can't spend all that money on stuff we don't even need."

"Let's keep it. Please, Cindy" Mollie glanced anxiously toward the back of the store where Richie was chatting with some customers. "Maybe Nicole will like it. Look—" She dug out one of the bright plates. "They're really cute."

"I don't know." Cindy frowned.

"Richie says they're very sophisticated."

"Who's Richie?"

"The salesman." Mollie smiled appealingly. "I told him all about the party, and he thought these were very appropriate. He suggested the matching tablecloth, too, and the dinner napkins and the cocktail napkins."

Cindy groaned. "He was being a good salesman, shrimp. He was drumming up sales."

"That's not true!" Mollie said indignantly. "He was very sincere."

"You dummy—you'd believe anything a cute boy told you."

"That's not true! Besides, he's very nice," Mollie said heatedly. "And I think he likes me."

Cindy rolled her eyes. "Not another instant crush! I thought you weren't over Paul yet—remember, your big summer romance?"

"Paul!" Mollie's eyebrows rose. "Paul has nothing to do with it. That was true love."

Cindy made a face.

"Well, first love, anyway," Mollie swore. "And besides, he lives in Quebec! One thing has nothing to do with another. Paul is in Canada, and Richie is right here."

"I can't believe my ears."

"Is there anything wrong with dating someone new?" Mollie folded her arms stubbornly.

"No," Cindy admitted. "But Richie isn't interested in you, squirt. He's too old, for one thing. He was probably just being polite."

Mollie grabbed the shopping bag, lifting it with difficulty. "You're wrong. You're wrong about everything—Richie and the decorations."

"Let's see what Mom says." Cindy marched to

the car, letting Mollie struggle with the shopping bag. "What next?" she muttered.

"You're wrong about Richie," Mollie insisted, climbing into the passenger seat. "You'll see, at the party. Richie's terrific, and he likes me, I know it."

"At the party? You didn't invite him, did you?" Cindy's eyes widened in alarm.

"Why not? I told you, he was very nice."

"No way!" Cindy shook her head. "You can't ask a total stranger! For one thing, it's not your party. It's Nicole's—and for her best friends only."

"I can ask a date if I want."

"No, you can't," Cindy insisted. "Mollie, we agreed. This is strictly for family and friends."

"Well, by that time Richie will be a friend. There's two days left until the party. Three, if you count Friday during the day."

Cindy gaped at her as though she'd lost her mind, making Mollie squirm uncomfortably. She had a feeling Cindy might be right.

Cindy turned the ignition key and started the motor. "Unbelievable! Mollie, a date is out. It would change everything. You can't have him, and that's that. Discussion ended."

"You're just saying that because Grant is in Hawaii," Mollie accused her sister. "If Grant were in Santa Barbara, you'd make darned sure that he was invited."

Cindy sighed in exasperation. "It's completely different. I've been going out with Grant for almost a year now, so he practically is family. Richie isn't going to know anyone there."

"But no one has to talk to him but me," Mollie pleaded.

"That's ridiculous. I think Nicole would rather you spent time with her than with a strange boy."

"She hasn't wanted to spend time with me all week," Mollie pointed out.

"That's true," Cindy agreed, "But still, the party is her last night home. We should save it for her."

"I guess," Mollie grumbled.

"So you'll tell Richie not to come?"

"I can't do that," Mollie protested. She scowled, then brightened. "I know! I'll tell him we already invited too many people, and he'll feel so bad about it, he'll have to ask me out."

"Doesn't follow," Cindy said curtly.

"Well then, I'll feel so bad I'll have to ask *him* out." Mollie looked at her sister hopefully.

"You're impossible." Cindy sighed.

"Well, what else am I supposed to do?" Mollie pouted.

"Just disinvite him."

"That's an awful thing to do."

Cindy eyed her sympathetically. "I know. But you should have thought of that before you asked him." She paused. "Go ahead—I'll wait."

"Now?" Mollie stared at her, horrified. "I can't do it now!"

Cindy relented. "Well, okay—not now," she agreed. "That would be embarrassing. But soon," she warned.

"Okay. But promise you won't tell anyone I asked him," Mollie begged.

"Oh, all right. But sometimes I wonder about your sanity."

Mollie was wondering about that herself. All the way home she stared out the window, her thoughts a jumbled mess. Inviting Richie had seemed like a great idea at the time. But now that she thought about it, she wondered if Cindy was right after all. Maybe Richie was just being a good salesman. Though he was awfully nice to her. And he had said "*au revoir*" instead of "good-bye."

Still, either way, she knew she had to withdraw her invitation. And that wasn't going to be easy. How did she get herself into these things?

Chapter 8

When the girls arrived home, the house was quiet. Cindy decided to get right down to work. She checked her list of names. She'd call Bitsy first—of all Nicole's friends, she knew Bitsy the best.

"*Bonjour, ma petite!*" Nicole sang out gaily as she bounced into the kitchen. Guiltily Cindy shoved the guest list behind her back.

"Nicole! You're up early."

"Not so early." Nicole gave her sister a curious look. "What mischief are you up to?"

"Nothing! I, uh ..." Cindy stammered. "Listen, you don't need the car, do you?"

Nicole filled a cereal bowl and took the milk from the refrigerator. "Yes, as a matter of fact, I do."

"Again!" Cindy pretended to be really annoyed. "I never get it anymore!"

"You had the car yesterday. But don't worry,"

Nicole said coolly, her good mood quickly fading. "A few more days and you can have the car all you want."

Nicole put the milk back, and Cindy managed to stash the party list away in a drawer. "Yeah, well—good," Cindy said.

Nicole looked at her strangely. "All you talk about is the car!"

"Well, it's important to me," Cindy said nervously. It seemed as if Nicole was taking forever to eat her cereal. When she finally finished eating, she took her bowl to the sink and rinsed it.

"Are you ever going to leave?" Cindy burst out.

"Don't worry." Looking offended, Nicole smoothed her skirt, then grabbed her pocketbook. "I'm out of here."

As Nicole left the kitchen, Cindy breathed a sigh of relief and rescued the party plans from their hiding place.

In the garage Mollie was busy making a mess as usual, pulling things down from the shelves. When Nicole said good morning to her, Mollie nearly jumped out of her skin.

"What's the matter with everyone?" Nicole said crossly.

"Nothing!" With one foot Mollie kicked the bag of party decorations farther behind her. Nicole didn't seem to notice it—but she did notice what Mollie was wearing.

"Aren't those my shorts?"

"Y-yes," Mollie stuttered, "but you said I could have them."

"I know, but . . ." Nicole seemed hurt. "Couldn't you wait until I was gone?"

Mollie stared at her blankly. "What for?"

Nicole sighed. "Oh, never mind." Angrily, she slammed into the car.

"Where are you off to?"

"None of your business," Nicole grumbled, pulling out of the garage.

Mollie watched her go. When Nicole was safely down the street, she stored the decorations on a shelf and pulled a stack of newspapers in front to cover it. They would be safe there until she decided what to do with them. Satisfied, she went into the kitchen.

"Nicole sure is crabby this morning," she complained. "What's with her anyway?"

"I don't know." Cindy scanned the list of people they were going to invite. "She sure is a pain, though."

"Really. And we're giving her a party?"

Cindy shrugged. "I guess we owe it to her."

"Not if she keeps this up." Mollie paused. "Of course, if we called it off, you or Mom could return the stuff to the party store."

Cindy gave her a knowing look. "Forget it, shrimp—that's your problem."

With a sigh of defeat, Mollie slumped into a kitchen chair. "All right—I'll take care of it. But I bet Mom says paper plates are a good idea. No washing up afterwards."

Cindy rolled her eyes. "Good luck. Now leave me alone so I can get this done." Cindy pulled the phone into the living room for some peace and quiet.

Quickly she dialed the first number. Bitsy answered right away.

"I realize this is short notice," Cindy said, explaining about the surprise party, "but I hope you can come."

Bitsy was surprised to hear from Cindy, but even more surprised to hear of the party.

"I know you just had a party," Cindy said, "but we didn't want to tell people, in case anyone spilled the beans."

"That's probably a good idea," Bitsy agreed. "Someone would have told Nicole, and it would have ruined the surprise."

"Right, and anyway, this is nothing like your barbecue," Cindy told her. "We're cooking a special French dinner. Just the family and some of Nicole's close friends—a special sit-down dinner."

"Is your mother cooking?"

"We all are."

"Count me in," Bitsy exclaimed. "I love anything your mom makes."

"Great!" Cindy checked off Bitsy's name.

"Who else are you inviting?"

Cindy read off her list, and Bitsy made sure she had all the right phone numbers. "I wonder ..." Bitsy hesitated.

Cindy guessed what she was thinking. "About Mark," she finished. "Is it silly to ask him? I mean, I know they broke up ages ago, but they're still friends."

"I know. But they hardly spent any time together at my party. In fact," Bitsy mused, "Nicole spent more time with Sean Elliot than with Mark."

"Really? I know him," Cindy exclaimed. "He surfs at our beach sometimes. I didn't know Nicole was friends with him."

"I don't think she was until yesterday."

"Well, we don't want to ask anyone new. This is a going-away party for special friends," Cindy pointed out. "Just the ones she'll miss the most."

"Better leave him out, then," Bitsy agreed. "Besides, he's really not her type."

"You can say that again," Cindy said; then she read through the list one more time.

"Sounds perfect," Bitsy told her.

"Great. I'll call everyone this morning."

"How are you going to keep it a secret?"

"I'm not sure," Cindy admitted. "But I'll think of some clever plan. Anyway, I'd better get going on these phone calls."

"Well, I'm sure everyone will want to come to the dinner," Bitsy assured her. "We're all going to miss Nicole."

"Me, too," Cindy declared. "She can be a pain sometimes, but I sure am going to miss her."

Nicole would have been astonished to hear those words. At the same moment that Cindy was hanging up the phone, Nicole was silently giving her sisters a piece of her mind. Here she was, petrified at the thought of leaving home, and her sisters couldn't care less! It really hurt. Mollie didn't even wait a second before wearing my old clothes, Nicole thought resentfully. I wouldn't be surprised if she moved into my bedroom the instant I'm gone. And Cindy's just as bad—all she cares about is getting the car! It would serve them right if I decided not to go away after all.

In fact, no one understood how she felt—except Sean. She was really looking forward to seeing him this morning. If she had second thoughts at all, they disappeared the instant she spotted him waiting on the curb outside his house. He looked so attractive, dressed in a casual shirt and rumpled white pants. It was thrilling to think this gorgeous guy was waiting for her!

Sean waved her into the driveway, and Nicole pulled up close to the garage, carefully locking the doors as she got out of the car.

"I would have picked you up," Sean said after they had exchanged greetings.

Nicole flushed. "I know, but this is better." Actually, she didn't know why she was keeping him a secret, but it seemed as though there would have to be too many explanations if he suddenly showed up at her house.

"Okay." Sean shrugged. "Anyway, I'm all set to go. How about you?"

"I'm ready." Nicole reached into her bag and took out the UCSB catalog Sean had loaned her the night before. "Here, you can have this back now."

"So—what did you think?"

"You were right—there are tons of great classes. I should have read it long ago."

Sean beamed. "That's what I keep telling you." He led the way to his car, which was parked by the curb. "I gave the Red Devil a bath this morning especially for you."

Nicole looked at the gleaming new car, then at the proud smile on Sean's face. "Well, thank you," she said with a grin. "He looks very ... very clean."

"Do you hear that, Red Devil?" Sean asked as

they climbed into the car. "You're a clean machine." With a purr the Red Devil started up. Sean
drove to the old overlook drive, a little-used road
with a spectacular view of the ocean. At first
Nicole wondered if the road was a shortcut,
but then Sean suddenly pulled to the side of
the road.

"Hawkins Cove," he said. With the engine running he pointed down at the shoreline. There was
a magnificent vista. "I love this place."

"Me, too," Nicole said, gazing at him in surprise. "But I haven't been here in years—I forgot
all about it. When I was little, I used to take
picnic lunches up here with my sisters."

"No kidding! Hey, maybe you saw me." He
grinned disarmingly. "I was the one on a bright
red ten-speed."

Nicole laughed. "Sorry—I don't remember."

"Well, it's probably a good thing you don't remember," Sean confessed. "I didn't like girls very
much back then."

"How about now?" Nicole asked lightly. She
realized she was flirting, and she blushed.

But Sean didn't seem to notice. He pulled out
and, as they drove on, kept busy pointing out
other favorite sights. "And here's the turnoff you
take to the art museum."

"You like the art museum?" Again, Nicole started
in surprise.

Sean acted offended. "Hey, I'm more than a
jock, you know."

"I know, Sean, I didn't mean that," Nicole said
quickly. "It's just a coincidence. I'm a member of

the museum. I always wanted to volunteer, you know, give tours—but I never had time."

"Sounds like you don't have time for lots of things."

"Maybe." Nicole frowned.

"Well, I'm not that involved with the museum," Sean admitted, "but I'm glad it's there when I feel like going."

"I know what you mean." Nicole studied his profile. "I didn't know we had so much in common."

"It's pretty wild," Sean agreed. "I never would have suspected. I mean you were . . ." He paused.

"The serious type," Nicole finished for him. "Maybe that was a mistake."

They stopped at a traffic light, and Sean looked at her curiously. Nicole felt her stomach flutter. Whenever Sean got that serious look, it did something to her insides. "Uh—we have the light," she said finally.

"Oh!" He broke into a grin. "Better go, then."

Arriving at campus, Sean stopped at the main gate, and the guard told them that the information they wanted was in the Admissions Building.

"Admissions? I only wanted to know about the French Festival," Nicole said.

"That's okay. You'll need your own catalog and application forms, too."

"Well, I'm still not sure about that." This time Nicole knew the fluttery feeling in her stomach was from nerves. Every time Sean talked about college, she felt completely unsure of herself.

Meanwhile Sean was giving her the grand tour, pointing out all the favorite gathering places on the attractive campus. Nicole had only been to

UCSB once or twice, but she thought now that she'd never seen a more beautiful campus. Overhead the sky was a brilliant blue, bringing out the colors of the lush flowers and the waving palm trees.

Nicole sighed. "This is nothing like Briarwood, especially the pictures I've seen of Briarwood in winter—all those bare trees and cold white snow...."

"Sounds brutal."

"Well, I have a new winter coat."

"You'll need more than that to keep you warm," Sean said lightly. "It sounds lonely. Cold and lonely."

Nicole frowned. Secretly she thought he was right. "I do hate to leave all this," she admitted.

Sean parked the car, and they walked to the Admissions Building. Every palm tree seemed to be waving at Nicole, saying good-bye. She shook her head, telling herself not to be so dramatic. She could always come home to visit.

In the foyer of the Admissions Building Nicole found a table with information about the French Festival. There was a concert that very night! She hurried over to the table where Sean was gathering papers.

"Look at this—a concert of Renaissance music, tonight! And films all day tomorrow. Let's see—my trunk is all ready, and most of my other things are already packed. I could go to a few of these things before I leave."

"Enough about leaving." Sean pushed a brand-new catalog and a stack of papers into her hands. "This will take care of that idea."

Nicole took a deep breath. Sean had handed her admission forms. "I don't know," she said.

"Just in case ... Like I told you last night, you could transfer here in a second. You should really think about it."

Outside, they sat on a sunny spot on the lawn while Nicole read through the catalog once more. "You're right. It isn't too late to apply. They sure make it easy on you here."

"Sure. It's not some stuffy eastern place."

Nicole glanced up. The wind was ruffling Sean's hair, just the way she liked. She felt that strange excitement again. *Am I just excited about the possibility of changing all my plans?* she wondered. *Sean makes it all sound so logical, I think he might be right.* Just then he caught her eye and smiled. Her stomach lurched. *Or maybe the excitement is Sean ...*

Shyly Sean moved his eyes away from hers. "Uh—how about the French classes?" He reached over to flip the pages of the catalog. Suddenly Nicole was afraid to breathe. Sean didn't seem to notice as he began reading the course titles out loud.

"Introduction to French History ... France between the Wars ... Hey, this sounds good—French Culture through Literature."

Nicole was staring at him. She couldn't help herself. There was something sweet about his face when he was relaxed. She could really imagine him as a little boy on his red bicycle.

"Nicole? You listening?" He glanced up at her. Their eyes met again.

Nicole stammered, "Oh, uh . . . I was just worried about changing plans so suddenly."

"Well, sometimes things happen that way."

Nervously she said, "Do they?"

She wasn't sure exactly how it happened, but the next thing she knew, Sean was kissing her, and she was kissing him back.

She pulled away, terribly confused.

"What's wrong?" Sean peered at her anxiously.

"Nothing! I mean . . . Sean, I don't want to lead you on. I'm supposed to be leaving in a few days."

"We talked about all that. You don't have to leave, Nicole."

She inhaled sharply. "Well," she said quietly, "what you say makes some sense. I mean, about spending freshman year close to home. College is change enough without going thousands of miles away."

"That's right. You can't argue with that."

Nicole grew thoughtful. She'd been up half the night, thinking it all through. She had been serious about her work in high school. She'd worked so hard, and look what had happened—she'd missed out on many friendships. She could have gotten to know Sean years earlier.

What if she went away to college and missed out again? Part of the college experience was meeting new people and doing new things. If she wasn't free to experience that, she'd miss half of what college was about.

She reached for the admission form. Sean smiled. "You're not going away," he said confidently.

"I'm not?"

"No way."

Nicole hesitated, but then she looked into Sean's blue eyes. "You're right," she said, surprised. "I'm not." She felt as if a huge weight had lifted from her shoulders. No fears of moving away from home, no worries of being a stranger in a new place. She felt wonderful!

Sean took her hand. "Things have a funny way of turning out, don't they?"

He kissed her again. Nicole felt breathless—and happier than she'd been in weeks! Flustered and excited, she bent over her college forms. Together, they filled everything out and carried them to the admissions office. After making arrangements to send in a copy of her high school transcript, Nicole left a small deposit. She and Sean left the building hand in hand.

"I can't believe it," she cried. "Bitsy will flip!"

Sean hugged her and Nicole closed her eyes. It felt so good to be in his arms. At last she felt sure of things again. She felt safe and protected. No more worries! Now she could look forward to the future.

Chapter 9

*L*ightly Nicole shut the door of the Red Devil. Over the top of the car, her eyes met Sean's, and the two of them stood silently for a long moment. It felt so good to be with someone special again. And while she and Sean were only starting out together, already she felt safe and secure just being near him. In fact, she wished they could stay this way forever, with all the newness and excitement of their first kiss to think about, and everything to look forward to. But there were other things to think about. Nicole glanced at her watch.

"Mon Dieu! Look at the time!"

"What's your hurry? What difference does it make?" Sean gazed at her.

"Lots, actually," Nicole admitted. "I wanted to stop by Bitsy's before I head home to change for the concert tonight."

"Bitsy, huh?" Sean looked pleased. "I guess you want to tell her the big news?"

Nicole nodded. *"Bien sûr."*

"I love it when you talk French," Sean said, walking around the car to take her hand.

Nicole was startled. "Oh! I didn't realize ..." She felt herself blush. All her close friends were used to her French phrases. But Sean was different. Somehow, it felt funny, using her favorite French expressions in front of him.

"Hey, what's wrong?"

Sean was peering at her in concern.

Nicole tossed her head and flashed him a smile. "Not a thing!" Anyway, she told herself, nothing worth worrying about now! Just wait until Bitsy heard her new plans!

Sean walked Nicole to her car, giving her a kiss on the top of the head as she slid into the driver's seat. "See you later," he said.

"Au revoir," Nicole replied softly. She gave one last look at his face, trying to memorize the curve of his smile. Sean closed her door and stood watching as she drove away.

Now Nicole couldn't wait to start college. She was so happy, she hummed as she drove. In her mind she was outlining her new plans. She'd unpack all her clothes, and of course, wire Briarwood to let them know she wasn't coming. She supposed they would refund most of her tuition check, but she wouldn't worry about that now. Anyway, her parents would end up saving a lot of money by sending her to a state school. They should like that, she thought. And I hope they like Sean! It looks like I'll be seeing a lot more of him.

He had been such a help that afternoon, especially when she'd decided that she might as well fill out her application forms right then and there. Sean was right; UCSB made things easy for her. In fact, the registrar had assured her that there should be no problems at all—Nicole had an excellent record. The praise made her feel good. But after all, she realized, her test scores and her school record had been good enough to get her accepted at Briarwood.

Briarwood. She couldn't help feeling the tiniest pang of remorse when she thought about it. Well, I'm only eighteen, she reasoned. I've got my whole life in front of me to go back East. I can even transfer to Briarwood next year if I want. But for now I'm happy staying right here in Santa Barbara!

At Bitsy's house Nicole parked and ran to the front door, poking her head inside as she rang the doorbell to call Bitsy's name. She was so excited, she could hardly wait to see her friend.

"Nicole—what are you doing here?" Bitsy appeared, dressed in an old T-shirt and faded cut-offs, with hot rollers covering one half of her head.

Nicole barely noticed how Bitsy looked. "I've got the best news," she crowed.

Bitsy's face lit up. "Great! Come into my room. I've got to finish my hair." Bitsy led the way down the hall to her spacious bedroom, which was littered with piles of washed and folded laundry—much as Nicole's room had been.

"Excuse the mess," Bitsy said, moving a pile of clothing to make room for Nicole on the bed.

"My room looked exactly the same."

"Oh, I guess your packing's all done." Bitsy nodded. "Have you sent your trunk yet?"

"It's going tomorrow morning. That is, it *was* going."

Bitsy transferred her rollers to the other side of her head and the newly curled hair fell over her face in bouncy ringlets. "What do you mean, *was*? You can't take it on the plane with you?"

"No, I can't." Nicole leaned back, hugging her knees. "But guess why not?"

"I don't know—hey, where have been been anyway?" Bitsy asked. "I tried to call you before."

"Come on, Bitsy—guess. It has to do with why my trunk isn't leaving tomorrow."

Bitsy stuck a bobby pin between her teeth. "You decided to wear all the clothes you can take."

"No. Oh, I can't tease you anymore. But it's a big surprise."

"Well, I love surprises." Bitsy plopped onto the bed. "What is it? A going-away present?"

Nicole nodded, a smile spreading across her face. "Yes—a kind of going-away present!"

"Well, where is it?" Eagerly Bitsy looked behind Nicole's back.

"Well, your present is—I'm not going anywhere."

"You're not?" Bitsy frowned, looking slightly bewildered. "Wait—I don't get it. You're not going this week, you mean? You're staying home a few extra days! That's great!"

"No, no—*pas du tout*," Nicole exclaimed, enjoying Bitsy's confusion. "You don't understand—I'm not going at all." She sat back, waiting for Bitsy's reaction.

"I don't get it."

"I'm not going to Briarwood. I've decided to go to the University of California, UCSB. Right in Santa Barbara!"

Bitsy shook her head. "But what happened? You were accepted; I saw the letter. . . . Briarwood was thrilled to have you."

Nicole laughed out loud. "It's nothing like that. Briarwood didn't suddenly reject me." The excitement and relief she felt as a result of her decision bubbled to the surface until Nicole was laughing so hard that tears came to her eyes.

Bitsy's eyes widened in alarm. "Are you all right, Nicole?" Her confusion only made Nicole laugh harder. Finally, she grabbed a tissue from Bitsy's night table and dabbed at her eyes. "You should see the look on your face," she gasped. "Don't worry, Bitsy—I'm not crazy." She cleared her throat and tried to explain calmly.

"I decided not to go away, that's all. I spent the day at UCSB; that's why I wasn't home when you called. They said it would be easy to transfer my records and everything. So I already left an application form and a deposit, and I can finish registering next week. Isn't it wonderful? I don't have to worry anymore, because I'm not going anywhere!"

Nicole expected Bitsy to jump up and down and squeal in delight. But instead, Bitsy just sat there, a quizzical look on her face.

"Bitsy, didn't you hear me? I'm not leaving—I'm staying right here in Santa Barbara. I'll only be just up the coast from Los Angeles, so I can visit you at UCLA whenever I want!"

Bitsy's mouth opened, but she couldn't seem to

get any words out. Finally, she said, "But ... why? What made you change your mind?"

"It just makes sense," Nicole said. Carefully she told her friend about her new plans. "And UCSB has some really solid courses," she finished.

"Really? In your major?"

"Oh, yes. I was surprised, too. But really, they're not bad at all."

"And you're going to stay there all four years?"

For the first time, Nicole hesitated. "I don't know. I guess I'll see how it goes," she said vaguely. "But definitely for the first year. Well, for first semester, anyway. By then I'll be used to college routine, and if I decide to transfer, it will be a lot easier."

"I guess so."

Now it was Nicole's turn to frown. "I thought you'd be ecstatic."

"I am—I guess."

"But you do agree, don't you?" Nicole looked at her seriously. "Everything I say makes sense, n'est-ce pas?"

"Well, I'm not sure," Bitsy answered. "I think you're saying that going to college here is less of an adjustment than going to Briarwood. But it's still college, so I don't see—"

"It's not the same," Nicole said impatiently. "At Briarwood I'd be from out of state. An oddball."

"But won't there be plenty of kids from out of state?"

"A few, I suppose. That's not the point," Nicole stated. "The point is, like Sean says—"

"Sean?" Bitsy interrupted, looking very surprised. "Sean Elliot?"

"Yes. Anyway, Sean says it's upsetting enough starting college without being new in town. Staying here is . . . less stressful. That's all I mean."

"Oh." Bitsy shrugged. "I guess that's kind of logical."

"It's very logical," Nicole stressed.

Bitsy picked up a brush and began to run it through the curly half of her head. "I didn't know you listened to Sean Elliot's advice. I thought you barely knew him."

"I didn't know him until yesterday," Nicole admitted. "And you know, I'm sorry. I wasted a lot of time in high school, when you think of it."

"How's that?"

"By working so hard. I missed knowing lots of great people, like Sean and like Cara Grossman and lots of others. I won't make that mistake again."

"You can't be friends with everyone," Bitsy pointed out. "You didn't waste time. You had a reason for working hard."

"What reason? To go away to school? I don't even want to. No, I'm changing my ways," Nicole said seriously. "Starting with getting to know Sean. Anyway, yesterday we really got to talking, and what he said made sense. He lent me his UCSB catalog last night and drove me to campus this morning."

"Sean helped you decide?"

Nicole nodded. "He's . . . he's great."

"This is awfully sudden."

Nicole's shoulders sagged. "I thought you'd be really happy. I thought you'd be pleased I was staying here."

"I am," Bitsy insisted. She became wistful. "I mean, having you around would be wonderful. A lot better than writing letters."

"Then, what's wrong?"

Bitsy shook herself. "Nothing. I'm—I'm happy for you. So, are you living at home or in a dorm?"

Nicole waved a hand in dismissal. "I haven't gotten that far yet. This is enough to hit my parents with. We'll figure the rest out later."

"Oh, I see." Bitsy nodded. "Then, they don't know yet. They won't like it, will they?"

Nicole shifted uneasily but suddenly brightened. "They always say that they just want me to be happy. Well, this will make me happy. So, once I explain everything, very calmly and logically, they'll have to agree."

"Maybe."

"And the timing is perfect," Nicole cried. "Mom told me not to make plans for Friday night. I think she and Dad are taking us all out to dinner. That's when I'll tell them! By Friday I'll have most of the details worked out."

"Oh, I see!" Bitsy suddenly smiled. Now it made some sense. Obviously, Cindy had roped Sean into helping with the surprise party after all. Somehow all of this had to do with Friday night. They were throwing Nicole off the track, Bitsy reasoned, by distracting her with this silly talk about transferring schools. Bitsy knew how hard Nicole had worked to get into Briarwood, and she knew her friend would never throw that away. She'd have to call Cindy later to find out what was going on. It seemed as though Nicole's sister had gone a bit too far with her plan. Meanwhile it was important not to let on about the surprise party. She decided to agree with anything Nicole said.

"If you're happy, I'm happy," Bitsy suddenly declared, giving Nicole a big hug.

"Thanks." Nicole felt very relieved. "That makes it okay, then." She paused. "So, what do you think of Sean?"

Bitsy sat across from Nicole. "He's fun. I always said that."

"He is, isn't he? I can't believe I almost missed out on knowing him."

"I never pictured you two together," Bitsy said honestly.

"Why not?"

"You're not the same type."

"That's not true," Nicole protested. Thoughtfully she reached over to fix a loose curler in Bitsy's hair. "Well, maybe it is a surprise to me, too," she admitted.

Nicole laughed and Bitsy joined in. "He is a nice guy."

Nicole hugged herself. "He's more than nice. I don't know when I've laughed so much! He's ... he's like a breath of fresh air. I feel like a different person when I'm with him."

"That's good, I guess," Bitsy said cautiously. She didn't want Nicole to get too carried away.

"What's wrong?"

"Nothing. Only it's a lot of change all at once." Bitsy laid a hand on Nicole's arm. "It's hard for me to take it all in."

"It isn't that big a change," Nicole insisted. "Not at all. I'm still going to college, just in a different place."

"You're right. Only you know what's best for you."

"It is best for me," Nicole agreed. "And besides, like Sean says, people should be spontaneous."

"Well, anyway, it's good to see you happy. You haven't been yourself lately."

Nicole threw her hands over her ears. "I wish people would stop saying that! This *is* myself! I can be fun too, you know. I'm a spontaneous person."

"I never said you weren't. Hey, I'm on your side." Bitsy gave Nicole a heartfelt hug.

Nicole smiled sheepishly. "I'm sorry. I guess I am a bit jumpy."

"Well, this is all pretty exciting, all this college stuff." Bitsy paused. "I can't believe we have another family party tonight. I'd ask you along, but ..."

Nicole jumped up. "Thanks, but I can't anyway." She glanced at the clock. "Sean's picking me up in an hour." She peered in the mirror, running Bitsy's brush through her hair.

Bitsy got up to walk her to the door. "Where to tonight?"

"The French Film Festival on campus." Nicole turned around. "Oh, Bitsy, won't it be great? Staying here, I mean. Imagine, I'll be going out with Sean, and you'll be so close. Maybe we could double-date!"

"Yeah, that would be nice."

"You know," Nicole confessed, "until I got to know Sean, I'd really missed having a boyfriend. You never have to worry about being lonely with a boyfriend."

Bitsy was about to remind Nicole that she would

easily meet new boys at her new school, but instead she said, "I don't want you to be lonely."

Nicole looked pleased. "And I'm so glad you agree with me. It makes everything easier."

"I guess so."

Nicole gave her friend one more hug. "I'd better run. I want to get the car back early. I need everyone on my good side right before I spill the news."

"Right. Well, good luck," Bitsy said cheerfully.

"Au revoir!" In high spirits Nicole picked her way down the gravel drive.

. . . .

Chapter 10

Cindy scanned her invitation list, feeling pleased—
everyone had accepted. All of Nicole's best friends
would be coming to the party.

"Ten acceptances, plus the five of us—that's a
lot of cooking," Cindy told Mollie. "I hope Mom
doesn't mind."

Mollie glanced up from her magazine. "Uh, better make that sixteen," she said hesitatingly, "in
case Richie comes."

"Richie!" Cindy whipped the magazine out of
Mollie's hands. "You still haven't told him? You
know he can't come."

Mollie made no move to grab the magazine
back from her sister. Instead, she flashed her
most winning smile. "You know, Cindy, I've been
thinking. . . ."

"That's dangerous," Cindy muttered.

Mollie even ignored that wisecrack. "See, I think

maybe we should keep those party things. You never know when we might need them again."

"Going-away decorations? Are you planning a trip, shrimp?"

Mollie refused to get annoyed. "I was even thinking, I could pay for them out of my allowance." She sighed involuntarily. "It is a sacrifice—I was saving for a few new albums."

"Mollie, just take the stuff back to the store."

"I can't," Mollie wailed.

"You have to, shrimp. Even if you keep the stuff, you'll still have to go there to tell Richie he can't come to the party."

"Please—couldn't you tell him?"

"No way. You got into this. It's about time you learned your lesson."

Mollie looked so genuinely miserable that Cindy felt sorry for her. "Oh, okay," she sighed. "I'll ask Mom if we can keep the stuff."

"And if we can, I won't have to go to the store," Mollie said hopefully. "Then I could call Richie and disguise my voice and say that Mollie was stricken with some awful disease, and the party is off."

Before Cindy could tell Mollie what she thought of *that* idea, they both saw the Moveable Feasts van pull up outside. Their mother jumped out, waving good-bye to her assistant, and let herself in through the kitchen door. "In here, Mom," Cindy called.

Laura Lewis dragged herself into the living room and collapsed on the couch. "Thank goodness I'm home!"

"You look beat," Mollie said sympathetically.

"The Deveres are impossible," their mother said. "Mrs. Devere is so picky. And Mr. Devere is even worse! He keeps reading about what other people have for anniversary parties and changing the menu. They're driving me crazy."

Mollie looked over at Cindy, pleading with her eyes for her sister to ask about the party decorations.

"Not yet," Cindy whispered. Out loud she said, "Mom, you need a nice hot cup of coffee," and she hurried into the kitchen.

"Thanks, Cindy," Mrs. Lewis said as she sipped the hot liquid. "I needed this."

Mollie whispered to Cindy. "Go on—ask her now."

"Not yet," Cindy answered, but their mother overheard.

"Ask me what?" She smiled weakly at them.

"Nothing bad," Cindy quickly assured her. "Just an idea, about Nicole's party. Mollie found these adorable paper plates and things that say 'goodbye' in four languages."

"Paper? Oh, I don't think so, hon."

"But paper plates are so much easier to clean up," Mollie reminded her. "We just throw everything out, even the tablecloth...."

"Washing up is no trouble at all with a dishwasher. No, I think Nicole will appreciate our using real china and linens. Her friends should like it, too. It's more special. Especially for fancy French food."

Cindy gave Mollie a meaningful look, and Mollie sighed. So much for easy outs. "I guess so," she agreed gloomily.

Mrs. Lewis drained her coffee and asked for

another cup. "And where's our party menu? We have to make a shopping list." She glanced at the page of notes Mollie handed her. "I already have some of these things in the shop."

"I can get the other groceries tomorrow," Cindy offered.

"You and Mollie will both have to," their mother said. "I've left the afternoon free, but I have to work in the morning. If you girls come in about lunchtime, we can have sandwiches together and get those éclairs started. They're the hardest, but we can make them ahead. We'll want to do the chicken Friday morning and the vegetables fresh, on Friday afternoon. Then we'll bring everything here at the last minute. Okay?"

"Okay," Cindy agreed.

"Mollie?"

Mollie looked up, startled. "Huh? Oh, sure. Whatever." She was too busy worrying about Richie to listen—how humiliating it would be to return all the decorations *and* disinvite him.

Their mother looked up. "Nicole doesn't suspect, does she? I want this to be a real surprise."

"It will be," Cindy promised. "Nicole hasn't paid us one bit of attention all week. She has no idea what we're planning."

"Really? Well, she's so busy getting ready for school, I suppose."

"Yeah, maybe."

Just then a car pulled into the garage. "There she is," Cindy said, taking the shopping list from her mother and stuffing it in the pocket of her jeans.

"Good," Mrs. Lewis said, "just in time for dinner."

Nicole shut the door gently behind her. "Hello, everyone."

"Don't you look nice—like a college girl already," her mother remarked.

"Thanks," Nicole said dreamily. Her eyes had a faraway look.

"Did you have a nice day with Bitsy, dear?"

"With Bitsy ... oh, yes," Nicole said. "Fine, thanks."

"Well, you'd better hurry and wash up. We'll eat as soon as your father gets in."

"Oh! Well, actually—I have plans for this evening. The French Festival at UCSB," Nicole said hurriedly. "You know, it's really a beautiful campus. I guess I never appreciated it before, living right here."

"You're not eating dinner here?"

"Sorry, Mother. I guess not."

Mrs. Lewis looked dismayed. "Nicole, we really haven't seen much of you lately."

"I know, but it's only dinner. You know, Mother, UCSB has some terrific programs. Like this French Festival. And their course listings are better than you might think."

"But, sweetheart, you're only home for two more days. It would be nice if you could spend a little more time here."

Nicole smiled mysteriously. "Well, it's really not a big deal. It won't matter, you'll see."

"I don't see." Now Mrs. Lewis looked really annoyed. "Are you all set to go? Done with your packing? You have everything you need to buy—"

"Don't worry so much! I have everything I need. But I'd better change. Sean is picking me up at ..."

Nicole colored. She hadn't meant to let his name slip.

"Sean! Sean Elliot?" Cindy gaped at her in surprise. "You're going out with him?"

"Just a casual date."

Mollie looked at her quizzically. "But why? Why start with a new boy when you're leaving in two days?"

"None of your business!" Nicole snapped, hurrying upstairs to change.

Mollie shrugged innocently. "What's she going out with him for?"

"Who knows?" Cindy griped. "I can't keep track of her moods."

Their mother sighed wearily. "Neither can I."

"I'm sure Nicole didn't mean to hurt your feelings." Cindy patted her mother's arm.

"I guess I'd better get used to it. Nicole's being gone, I mean. I might as well start now." She pulled herself up from the couch. "I'll take a rest before dinner."

When she had gone, Mollie said, "Mom really feels bad, doesn't she?"

"Our sister's a rat," Cindy announced. "But at least she didn't ask for the car again. Hey, maybe the party store is open late and you could take the stuff back tonight?" She turned brightly to Mollie, who suddenly busied herself straightening up the living room.

"Why don't I make dinner?" she volunteered.

"Defrost it, you mean."

"Whatever. And I'll clean up, too, as a special treat for Mom."

Somehow, after all Mollie's cooking and cleaning, there was no time left to go to the party store.

"Look at the time," Mollie exclaimed as she put the last clean plate into the cupboard. She yawned and stretched. "Bed for me."

Cindy eyed her sharply. "Gee, that's too bad, shrimp. I guess you'll have to go to the party store first thing in the morning."

Pretending she didn't hear, Mollie headed up the stairs.

Chapter 11

*T*hursday morning Nicole entered the kitchen just as Mollie and Cindy were finishing breakfast. She grabbed a cup of coffee.

Cindy eyed Nicole's fresh sundress and carefully applied makeup. "Another date with Sean?"

"Not a word, Cindy," Nicole warned.

"Then I'm right—you are going to see him. Talk about overexposure."

"Cindy, I warned you."

"Okay, okay. I don't care, as long as we have the car for once, I'm happy."

"I couldn't care less about the car," Nicole told her. A horn sounded outside. "That's him." Nicole put her cup down and started for the door.

"What's the rush?" Cindy eyed her curiously. "You act like you don't want him to come in."

"That's ridiculous, *idiote*. Of course he can come in." Nicole flung open the kitchen door and beckoned to him.

102

"Hi, Sean," Mollie greeted him when he'd walked through the door. "Hey, great T-shirt!"

Nicole looked at Sean's crazy psychedelic T-shirt and bright surfer shorts. "That's what you're wearing?"

"Why? Is this formal?"

Nicole glanced down at her favorite summer dress. "No, you're fine."

"Good," Sean replied, " 'cause it's going to be hot in that auditorium. I came prepared."

"You're staying indoors?" Cindy exclaimed. "On this gorgeous day? Perfect surfing weather."

"There are other things besides surfing," Nicole declared.

"Like what?" Cindy looked scandalized, and Sean laughed.

Nicole frowned at both of them. "Like French *cinéma*," she answered, using the French pronunciation.

Sean nodded at the coffee machine. "Is that fresh?" He helped himself while Nicole watched impatiently. "I'll need this, for a day of *cinéma*." He imitated Nicole's pronunciation, making a face at Cindy. Everyone laughed except Nicole.

"Let's go, Sean," she said, but he had already started talking to Cindy about surfing.

"On Saturday, I'm trying Bellisino Point."

"You are?" Cindy gazed at him in awe. "That's wicked surf."

"I'm sure this is fascinating," Nicole interrupted, "but we've really got to go." She opened the door and gestured for Sean to follow. *"Au revoir."*

"Au revoir, you all," Sean called.

"He's great," Cindy said, watching them leave. "And a real hunk."

"Right," Mollie agreed. "So why did Nicole act like she was embarrassed by him or something?"

"I thought so, too. I wonder why she's going out with him anyway?"

"Face it," Mollie sighed. "Our sister's weird."

"Not weirder than you," Cindy said cheerfully. "Put down the coffee, shrimp—time to face the music."

Unhappily Mollie fetched the party decorations from their hiding place in the garage and got into the car. Her stomach churned. What if she got sick in the store, in front of everyone? Cindy was cruel, refusing to help her out of this spot. She almost seemed to be enjoying Mollie's discomfort. Luckily, just as Cindy went to take the turn toward the party store, Mollie had a brainstorm.

"Wait," she cried. "We should do the shopping first. Just in case. We'll still have time to swing by the store afterward."

"Fortunately for you," Cindy told her, "that makes some sense."

Mollie leaned back in relief.

"But don't get too comfortable—you'll have to face him sooner or later." Humming a cheerful tune, Cindy headed for the supermarket.

To Mollie's delight they had to go to two more stores to find some of the more exotic vegetables and herbs her mother wanted. They ran so late, they had to rush to the catering shop.

"Your lucky day," Cindy said in disbelief. "There's no time now to go see Richie and return those things."

Mollie smiled for the first time all morning. "I knew something good would happen."

"Don't count your chickens before they're hatched," Cindy warned her. "You still have to go later."

"I know that."

"Don't think that you got away with anything."

"Okay, already. What are you being so hard on me for?"

"I'm not. You should just clean up your own messes."

"I will. I'll do it later."

"Well, don't take my head off."

"You're the one. It's none of your business anyway."

By the time they got to the catering shop, they were barely talking.

"Where's Mom?" Cindy started unloading the groceries where Barbara, their mother's assistant, directed them.

"With the Deveres—another emergency meeting! Your mom's over there now, but she said to tell you your lunch is in the kitchen, and you should start without her."

"You mean, start eating without her?" Cindy tucked the endive and radiccio behind some cartons in the large cooler.

"No, I mean start cooking without her."

"You're kidding! Barbara, you'll help, won't you? We don't know how to make éclairs."

"Sorry, kids—I'm running, too. Got to deliver these cakes to a client and stay to oversee her birthday party. You guys are on your own. Have fun." Staggering under a stack of cakes, Barbara backed out the door.

Mollie and Cindy exchanged panicked looks. "Oh, no," Mollie groaned.

"Well, look at it this way," Cindy said grimly. "At least you won't be going to any party store. We've got cooking to do."

"Let's eat first." Mollie plowed through the cooler, taking out the sandwiches marked for their lunch. "This looks delicious."

"Food is the last thing we need," Cindy griped. "And what about your diet? Your latest diet, I mean."

"Give me a break," Mollie cried, insulted. "I'm hungry."

Cindy found the instructions Mrs. Lewis had left them. "Think again—this is enough to make you lose your appetite." She read the éclair recipe out loud, then shook her head in despair. "Forget it—it's hopeless."

"Oh, well. We have to try." Mollie tied on an apron. "Maybe Mom will get back soon and save us."

"Well, okay," Cindy said doubtfully. "I'll start the dough. You do the custard filling."

Measuring carefully, Cindy poured one cup of flour into a stainless steel bowl, then added salt and sugar. "So far, so good. Now some butter and milk."

She measured those into a pot and mixed them well before setting the pot onto the stove.

"This isn't so hard," she bragged to Mollie. "I just let it come to a boil, then pour in the flour mixture, like the recipe says."

But the flour immediately turned into hard little lumps. Cindy glanced quickly at Mollie, but her sister was so absorbed in her own cooking that she hardly noticed what Cindy was up to. So,

Cindy added some more milk and whipped everything together. The lumps disappeared, but now it looked too watery!

Thinking fast, Cindy grabbed the pot off the heat, and set it aside while she fetched more flour from the canister. More flour ought to make it nice and thick, she reasoned. She added a generous amount and put the pot back on the heat for a little more cooking.

"Oh, no," Mollie cried suddenly.

"What's up?" Confident that her own problem had been solved, Cindy hurried to Mollie's side.

"I don't know," Mollie cried. "I put in the four cups of milk so there would be custard for twelve pastry shells," she began.

"Twelve? I'm making twenty-four." Cindy rolled her eyes impatiently. "You need twice that much!"

"Oh. Well, it doesn't matter anyway, because it's all ruined," Mollie finished glumly.

"But how?"

"It says add four beaten egg yolks, and I put in the whole eggs."

"You'll have to do it over."

"But how am I supposed to separate eggs?"

Cindy sighed. "Get more eggs, and I'll show you how."

"Since when do you know?" Mollie asked, returning from the cooler with eight eggs. At least this time she remembered to double the recipe, she thought, watching closely as Cindy tried to pour the egg white off the top of the opened shell. Unfortunately Cindy ruined more eggs than she separated.

"This is tougher than it looks," Cindy grumbled. Finally, though, she had eight egg yolks, with not too much white mixed in, and she beat them energetically into a frothy foam. "Where's your double boiler?" she asked Mollie.

"There." Mollie pointed to the stove where her other egg mixture bubbled gently.

"That's not a double boiler, that's a pot."

"What's the difference?"

Cindy gave Mollie a superior look. "The difference is that a double boiler cooks over boiling water," she explained, as if talking to a child.

"Well that's okay, then, because I didn't use any water."

"You don't put your water inside," Cindy began, but then the milk started bubbling over the top of the pot.

"Oh, no! What a mess." Mollie grabbed the pot and dropped it into the sink, where it hissed and sputtered.

"This is a disaster," Cindy cried.

"Uh, Cindy, I still smell something cooking."

"What? No, you ... oh no! My pastry dough!" Cindy ran to the stove and cautiously peered inside the pot. "It's okay, I think," she announced. Just to play it safe, she turned off the heat.

"Okay, now I have to add four or five eggs, beating each time," she muttered.

Patiently Cindy followed the recipe, beating in each egg after adding it. " 'The dough should stand erect when scooped up with a spoon,' " she read. " 'Use dough at once.' "

Doubtfully she stared at the sticky mess stuck to her spoon. Is this what it's supposed to look like? she wondered, shouting for Mollie to open the oven. "I'm supposed to bake these at once."

"Don't yell at me," Mollie answered. She peered into Cindy's pot. "That doesn't look like éclair shells to me," she said indignantly. "Aren't you supposed to roll it out flat?"

"Oh! I guess you're right." Cindy scooped the dough out of the pot and tried to pat it into shape with a spatula. But the dough lay on the counter, a gooey gray mess.

"I'm all done," Mollie gloated. "This time it's perfect, see?" She put her pot on top of the stove and lifted a spoonful.

Cindy sputtered with laughter. "Perfect? It's supposed to be a liquid filling!"

Dismally Mollie watched as her beautiful custard hung from the edge of Cindy's spoon. "So, it's a little thick. What's wrong with that?"

"But it's not supposed to be thick, Mollie."

"So what, at least it's better than your pastry."

"It is not!"

"Is too!"

Disgusted with this screaming match, Cindy assumed a haughty air. "It doesn't matter anyway. Nobody can eat this."

Tears came to Mollie's eyes. "It's not my fault."

"Well, it's not mine," Cindy swore.

Mollie tore off her apron. "Well, everyone knows I can't cook. I didn't want to do this anyway."

"No," Cindy taunted, "you wanted to go to the party store and see Richie."

Mollie's eyes widened. "Leave him out of it."

"Why? Obviously he's part of the problem. You're so busy dreaming about Richie, you can't keep your mind on anything." It felt so good to yell, Cindy didn't bother to worry if she was being fair or not.

"That's not true!"

"And I'm telling you, Mollie, if he shows up tomorrow night, you'll ruin everything."

"He won't show up! Oh, forget it. This party is nothing but trouble. I wish there wasn't any stupid party."

"We agree on that." Cindy flung off her apron and headed for the door.

"Where are you going?"

"Anywhere," she declared furiously. "I've had enough, too. I'm doing what I should have done in the beginning—I'm going surfing."

"I'm not staying here alone!"

"You're not going with me, 'cause I'm history!" Cindy banged out of the kitchen.

Mollie stood frozen to the spot, hardly believing it when she heard Cindy roar off in the car. She was stranded! Furiously she grabbed her pocketbook and slammed out of the kitchen, stopping only to lock the front door behind her and put the CLOSED sign on the door.

It wasn't her problem. She would just have to take the bus to the mall to cool off. She was far too angry to cook. And she was certainly too angry to face Richie, and besides—Cindy had the party things in the car. She couldn't have returned them even if she wanted to!

The rest of the afternoon Mollie spent happily wandering about the mall. She found a darling sweatshirt on sale, and went home eager to show it to everybody, totally forgetting about the disastrous éclairs.

As Mollie breezed in the door that evening, she

saw Cindy sitting stiff faced in the living room. Mrs. Lewis was sitting on the couch, her arms crossed, a stern look on her face.

"And where have you been, young lady?"

Suddenly Mollie's memory returned. "Uh," she stammered, "uh, at the mall."

"I'm furious with you both! I break my back to get away from the Deveres, to find a huge mess at the shop, and both of you gone."

"Well, I would have cleaned up," Mollie declared, "but Cindy didn't."

"Don't put all the blame on me," Cindy objected.

"But you were the first to leave."

Mrs. Lewis put her hands over her ears. "Quiet, both of you."

Mollie gritted her teeth. "I'm sorry, Mom. We can try again tomorrow," she offered.

"I've already made the éclairs." Her mother sat grimly, her lips pressed together angrily. "You were both wrong to leave the place a mess. This party for Nicole is a wonderful idea, but you've each got to do your share of the work."

"If it's anyone's fault," Mollie defended herself, "it's Nicole's."

"Nicole!" Mrs. Lewis was too surprised to criticize.

"Yes," Mollie insisted. "If she wasn't so grumpy lately, we would both be in a better mood and we wouldn't have argued, or made a mess, and you wouldn't be mad at anyone."

"Now I've heard everything." Mrs. Lewis threw up her hands.

"And what's more," Mollie continued, "she doesn't deserve a party. She's been horrible lately."

"Mollie's right," Cindy complained. "I mean, we're doing good deeds while Nicole is snapping at us and—"

"Shhh! Here she comes."

They all stopped to listen to the sound of a key in the front door. Nicole came in, and seeing everyone assembled there, held up a hand.

"Before anyone says a word," she warned, "I'm not in a very good mood. I didn't have a great day." She headed for the stairs. "I'll be in my room."

"See?" Mollie smiled triumphantly.

Mrs. Lewis frowned. "Just a minute, Nicole. I'd like to talk to you."

"I don't want to talk to anyone." Nicole looked as if she was going to cry.

Mrs. Lewis simply sighed. "Go ahead upstairs," she said.

"That's too much," Mollie declared. "She's hurt our feelings all week, and she doesn't care a bit."

"Now, Mollie," Mrs. Lewis cut in, "don't be too harsh, she has a lot on her mind."

"So do I." With a determined snort, Mollie tramped up the stairs after Nicole. She had half a mind to give Nicole a good telling off. But one look at her sister's red eyes, and Mollie hesitated. She felt a burst of sympathy.

"What do you want?" Nicole snapped. "I told you, Mollie, I don't want to talk."

Mollie's sympathy dwindled. "Well, excuse me. But you're allowed to give everyone a hard time? You have no consideration for anyone's feelings, and—"

"Consideration," Nicole nearly shrieked. "You come barging into my room! That's consideration?"

"Forget it. To think we were giving you a party—" Mollie gasped and clapped a hand over her mouth, but it was too late.

"What? What party?" Nicole sat bolt upright.

Mollie groaned. "It was supposed to be a surprise. Now Mom will really be furious with me."

"Wait a minute. I won't tell Mother if you explain exactly what you're talking about," Nicole ordered.

Reluctantly Mollie told her all about the fancy dinner they were planning for the next night. And she made sure that her sister knew how everyone was feeling a bit neglected, especially as it seemed that lately Nicole would rather spend her last days at home with Sean Elliot than with her own family.

"Poor Mother," Nicole said thoughtfully. "I didn't know she felt that way."

"We all do," Mollie declared.

Nicole stared at her. "Look, I have a phone call to make. Do you mind?"

Mollie jumped up. "I was only trying to help," she said indignantly.

The instant she left, Nicole crept out to the telephone in the hallway and dialed Bitsy's number. "Hi—are you busy? It's an emergency. I need to see you right away."

Chapter 12

*B*itsy let Nicole in and ushered her upstairs to her bedroom. "What's the big mystery?" she asked, flopping comfortably onto the bed.

"Oh, Bitsy," Nicole exclaimed. "I'm so confused."

"Uh-oh, you look bad." Bitsy grabbed the box of tissues and handed them to Nicole, just in case. "What happened?"

"It's just—we had such a terrible day together. He made wisecracks all through the films. Nothing but bad jokes! I really wanted to see them, and he didn't understand. We didn't get along at all."

"You mean Sean?" Bitsy interrupted.

"Of course! He had a better time chatting with Cindy about surfing! I think I made a big mistake."

Bitsy looked strangely unconcerned. "Oh. Well, that's nothing."

"Nothing!" Nicole blinked at her. "How can you say that?"

Bitsy seemed embarrassed. "Well, I just mean, it's hard to take it all seriously, that's all."

"Why? I do." Nicole looked at her in confusion. "Are we talking about the same Sean?"

"Sean Elliot, right?"

"Yes, Sean Elliot!" Nicole cried. She stared at her friend, but Bitsy seemed more interested in a loose thread hanging from the bedspread. "Bitsy, I thought I really liked him, and now I don't know what to think."

"Nicole, I don't know what to do. I'm not supposed to tell." She looked up at Nicole, distress showing in her face.

A light suddenly dawned in Nicole's mind. "Is this about my surprise party?"

"You know about it?" It was Bitsy's turn to look surprised.

"Mollie spilled the beans. But it's not her fault," Nicole rushed to add. "Actually I'm glad she did. But what's that got to do with Sean?"

"Everything, I thought. Wasn't he supposed to distract you? I mean, I didn't for a minute think you really liked him."

"Of course I liked him. What do you think I've been ranting and raving about?"

"But I thought ... Cindy said ..." Bitsy was at a loss for words.

"I'm more confused than ever," Nicole declared.

"Okay, I'll try to explain." Bitsy sat on the edge of the bed and took a deep breath. "When Cindy told me about the party, she said she'd think of some way to keep you in the dark. I'd mentioned to her that you seemed friendly with Sean at my barbecue, so I thought he had something to do with it. Like maybe he was supposed to keep you too busy to notice what was going on."

At first Nicole didn't say anything. She felt as if someone had kicked her in the stomach. Then, he never liked me? she thought. But what about his kisses—was he acting, the whole time? Nicole flushed angrily. "I'll kill Cindy! How could she do this to me?"

"Wait," Bitsy said, alarmed. "Look, I'm going to call Cindy right now and clear this up." While Bitsy went to the phone, Nicole threw herself onto the bed, her thoughts in turmoil.

If Sean was only acting, he certainly did a good job. And I let myself fall for him! I bet he's laughing himself silly right now. Nicole felt sick.

"Mystery solved," Bitsy announced, returning with a relieved smile on her face. "Cindy had nothing to do with it. Sean was for real."

"How do you know?"

Patiently Bitsy repeated everything Cindy had told her. Sean had no part in any schemes. In fact, Cindy never had a scheme.

"None at all?"

"None. But she did say she couldn't figure you and Sean together."

"I'm wondering about that myself," Nicole admitted. "You didn't give me away, did you?"

"No way. I was very casual. In fact, Cindy was nervous that we were talking about you behind your back. She had no scheme, believe me."

"That's a relief." Nicole sighed. "But it's still a mess."

"Then you don't like Sean?"

"I thought I did, but I don't, not after today. We really have different interests."

"I could have told you that," Bitsy said. "He's not for you."

"I see that now," Nicole said sheepishly. "And he's certainly no reason to give up my college plans," she added. "What a mistake I almost made! I really acted like an idiot, didn't I?"

"No, you didn't." Bitsy patted her hand. "Sean's real cute, and you were nervous about going away. I understand. Everyone's nervous."

"They are?"

"Sure. I'm nervous, and I'm only going a couple of hundred miles away, not three thousand." Bitsy sighed. "To be honest, I envy you, going so far away."

"Why? It's going to be so hard! All the adjustments, making new friends, being an outsider ..."

"Don't worry so much," Bitsy advised. "You could've had a much better time in Quebec this summer if you hadn't spent all your time worrying. You *can* handle it, Nicole. Just have faith in yourself. It's worth it."

Nicole frowned. "Do you really think so?"

"Absolutely."

"But now what do I do? I mean, do I stay or do I go?"

Bitsy looked at her in surprise. "Why on earth would you stay? Really, Nicole, I thought that was part of Cindy's plan. I never took this UCSB business seriously for a minute."

"But you agreed with me," Nicole pointed out.

"Only because of the party."

Nicole pursed her lips and exhaled a long stream

of air. "*Alors*, this is a mess. I guess I lose my deposit at UCSB."

"It could have been worse," Bitsy reminded her. "You could have actually gone there. For you, that would have been a bad mistake. You planned and dreamed about Briarwood. How could you not go?"

Nicole shrugged. "It seemed to make so much sense. I was really relieved about staying here."

"A bad case of leaving-home jitters. But don't ruin things for yourself." Bitsy shook her head thoughtfully. "I should have told you the truth all along."

"It's not your fault," Nicole said earnestly.

"But now you're going to break it off with Sean."

"*Oui, c'est la vie*," Nicole said lightly, feeling more like her usual self. "I guess I see now that he didn't have much to do with it, anyway. I was desperate for a way out of leaving home, so I latched on to him. It was unfair. He really deserves better."

"That's the old you talking," Bitsy said approvingly.

"Well, I've been acting pretty dumb."

Bitsy grinned. "That's okay. You were kind of cute. You're usually so much in control, it's almost a relief to see you make a mistake. I sure make enough of them."

"That's not true," Nicole said loyally. "Anyway, I'm far from perfect—this proves it. Oh, Bitsy," she exclaimed, "I'm so glad I have you to talk to. What will I do without you?"

They hugged, misty-eyed.

"Hey, maybe you can stay for supper tonight," Bitsy said at last.

"Oh, no!" Nicole closed her eyes. "I'm supposed to have dinner with Sean tonight. And we had a date for tomorrow, too."

"That's no good."

"I know. Well, I'll see him tonight, to explain. I owe him that. But I'll have to break that date for tomorrow, though. Can you believe, I actually thought I'd be making the big announcement at the party, telling everyone I was staying here to go to UCSB with Sean? I must have been crazy."

"Temporarily." Bitsy grinned.

"I'd better go home and get ready."

"Well, don't worry," Bitsy assured her. "Sean's a pretty nice guy. I think he'll understand."

"I hope so," Nicole muttered. "Sometimes I barely understand myself."

The ringing phone jolted Nicole out of a sound sleep. It's Sean, she thought in a panic, then relaxed. Memories of their date the night before flooded in on her. It hadn't been easy, but she had told him the whole truth. She explained how confused she was about school. She said she had really enjoyed being with him but had to admit they were not right for each other after all.

Sean was surprised at first, but then he just said he was sorry things hadn't worked out. He even suggested they see each other on vacations, to make sure they were doing the right thing.

The funny thing was, Nicole was already sure. Bitsy had been right about Sean. He was very friendly and helpful, and he did have a certain way about him that she really liked—but that special something just wasn't there. Things had

gotten out of hand. If it hadn't been for her confusion over college, they would never have gotten
together at all. She didn't tell Sean any of that, of
course. But secretly Nicole hoped she might meet
a boy with that special something at Briarwood.

But now the telephone rang again. Nicole dashed
into the hall and grabbed the receiver. "Madame
Preston!" she cried in surprise.

Her former French teacher apologized for the
early hour. "But could you possibly meet me at
school this afternoon? I've been putting new textbooks away in the storage closet, and I found
something you might be interested in."

"An old paper of mine?" But Madame Preston
refused to answer. Intrigued, Nicole agreed to
meet her at two o'clock. "*Au revoir*," she said
gaily, hanging up. It would be nice to have another chance to say good-bye to her favorite
teacher.

Downstairs Nicole found an empty house, but
on the kitchen table was a scribbled note in her
mother's handwriting:

*Nicole—all gone out. Dad, the office. Me, emer-
gency catering job. Cindy, surfing. Molly, mall.
BE SURE TO BE HOME FOR DINNER, six o'clock.
This is an order!*
Love, Mom
*P.S. Madame Preston called last night while you
were out. Said she'd call back.*

If Nicole hadn't known about the surprise party,
she would have believed every word. But she
suspected the note was a cover-up—all except

for the message from Madame Preston. No doubt the emergency catering job was her own French dinner, and Mollie and Cindy had been recruited to help.

Pleased to be the center of so much attention, Nicole hummed as she toasted two slices of bread and made a cup of coffee.

"I wish I hadn't gotten in so late last night," she told Cinders as the cat jumped onto her lap. "I've got a lot of apologizing to do. I have a feeling Mollie wasn't exaggerating when she said that I've been snapping at everyone lately." Thoughtfully, Nicole stroked the cat's fur. "But that will have to wait for tonight. Oh, Cinders, I can't wait to act surprised!"

With one last stroke Nicole set the cat down and went upstairs to shower and dress. A little while later she grabbed her old bicycle from the garage. The sun was bright, but there was a brisk breeze. A glorious day! She couldn't help feeling sentimental, and she decided to take a long ride to the beach before heading for the high school. No matter how wonderful college was, she would never forget all of this.

Chapter 13

"*C*indy parked the car. "Don't be long."

"Don't worry." Mollie grabbed the bag of party decorations from the back seat. "I won't be long," she said with a haughty air.

Bravely she faced the party store. She was so nervous, she felt sick to her stomach. How was she going to do this? Maybe, she thought hopefully, Richie won't be there! It could be his day off. Then she could leave a note and run.

Why did she have to face this anyway? It wasn't fair. She was only trying to help. She only bought the decorations to make the party better. And inviting Richie wasn't the crime Cindy made it out to be. If Cindy were a decent human being, she would understand.

But there was no way out. She had put it off and put it off, and now she had to go through with it. Cindy was waiting. She thought of the note they had left for Nicole that morning, saying she was at the mall shopping. If only the note were true. If only she were off shopping instead of disinviting a boy she hardly knew to a party she almost wished she wasn't having.

Besides being nervous, she was also feeling guilty for spilling the beans about the surprise party. So far, no one knew, but still she had to be on her best behavior. If she lost her cool, or if Nicole didn't act surprised enough, she'd be ruined. No one would ever trust her again. So she had to face Richie to prove what a responsible person she was. Oh, why was everything so complicated?

At the door to the party store, Mollie paused, taking a deep breath for courage. She could see Richie inside. Her heart sank. It wasn't his day off. She held her head high, pretending to be braver than she really was, and marched inside the store. Richie was filling a drawer with wrapping paper. Mollie hesitated, then tapped his arm.

"Hi. Remember me?"

He looked over his shoulder. "Hey, the French chef, sure. So how's it going?"

"Okay." She gave him a bright smile. "Well, not really okay. Uh, it turns out, my sister, uh, she, well ... we can't use these plates and things." She thrust the shopping bag at him.

He stood up slowly, looking grim and disapproving. "What do you mean?"

Mollie gulped. "I have to return these." Suddenly she felt a stab of terror. "They are returnable, aren't they? I didn't open anything."

Richie sighed. "Listen, do me a favor—you see that guy at the register?"

There was an old, balding man at the front counter. "Yes. I see him."

"Well, let him write it up, okay? I'm trying to get out of here early. I'm taking a long weekend, starting now."

Mollie wasn't sure she'd heard correctly. "You are? You mean, you're going away?"

"Anything wrong with that?"

"No! Of course not!" She tried not to stare. "But ... but what about ... the party?" she stammered.

He looked at her blankly. "Huh?"

Molly wet her lips. "Nothing. I mean ... you're leaving tonight?"

"Sooner—as soon as this stock is put away."

"Then you'll be gone this evening?"

Richie peered at her curiously. "That's right. Going camping. That is okay with you, isn't it?"

"Oh! Of course! I mean, that's wonderful! Then you won't be around tonight at all."

"Yeah. That's what I just said."

He was looking at her strangely.

"Oh, well ... camping is great. Have a great time; have a wonderful time."

He was going away. He hadn't even remembered about the party. Here she was so upset because she had to disinvite him, and he hadn't paid the least bit of attention. She was off the hook! If he wasn't coming, she didn't have to disinvite him. Thank goodness she hadn't mentioned her invitation! He wouldn't have known what she was talking about. Still, it was insulting. He hadn't taken her seriously, not for one minute.

She flounced toward the cash register. Well, he

wasn't half as cute as she remembered anyway. Let him go camping—she couldn't care less.

"What'll it be, miss?" The elderly man at the register smiled kindly at her.

"These things I bought ... well, I can't use them after all," she told him in her sweetest voice. "I'm sorry."

"A return?"

"Yes, please. Our plans have changed, and I'm afraid we can't use these things."

"No problem." Smiling, he processed a credit for her.

Mollie breathed a sigh of relief. "Thank you," she said. At least they had taken the stuff back without a hassle. She walked out to the parking lot, waving the credit slip.

"I got it!"

"Hooray." Cindy started the motor and backed up. "Thank goodness that's over. Was it bad?"

"It was hard," Mollie admitted.

Cindy glanced at her sympathetically. "What did Richie say?"

"Not too much," Mollie admitted. She couldn't help smiling—she was just so relieved the whole thing was over with.

Cindy patted her arm. Mollie was taking this awfully well. In fact, she didn't look upset at all.

"Were you embarrassed, shrimp?"

"Me?" Mollie shrugged. "Why should I be embarrassed?" Mischievously she glanced at her sister. "But I think he was pretty disappointed," she said.

Cindy's eyes opened wide. "Really?"

"Don't act so surprised," Mollie cried indignantly. "He could have really liked me. And I felt terrible that he couldn't come tonight. He said he'd ... he'd go away, camping for the whole weekend. I guess he was really disappointed. I hope I didn't break his heart or anything." She shook her head sadly.

Cindy shrugged. "I'm sorry, shrimp. I never thought he'd go for you. Guess I was wrong."

"That's okay," Mollie said grandly. "We all make mistakes."

Cindy frowned. "I'm sorry I made you do it. I hope you're not too disappointed."

Mollie was thoughtful for a minute. "Actually, Cindy, I think you were right. He was too old for me. I'd be bored with him." She glanced out the window at the party shop, then turned back to Cindy. "So, what are we waiting for? We promised Mom we'd help cook today, and we can't let her down again."

Cindy gazed at her sister in admiration. This was not the Mollie she knew. But it wasn't a bad Mollie, either. Maybe her little sister was growing up at last.

She pulled away from the curb and headed for Moveable Feasts. With their mother in charge, there would certainly be no more cooking disasters. Mrs. Lewis quickly had them in aprons and hard at work. With chicken and vegetables and chocolate mousse to attend to, the rest of the morning flew by.

Nicole carefully folded back the wrapping paper. "Oh, Madame—it's beautiful!" Her breath caught in her throat. *"Merci beaucoup."* Nicole stared with pleasure at the old French dictionary. It was covered in soft leather and engraved in gold. She glanced at her teacher. "You didn't really find this in the closet?"

"Not really," Madame Preston admitted. "I had it at home and suddenly realized it was the perfect going-away gift for you. It once belonged to my French teacher, so I'm continuing the tradition and passing it on to my favorite student."

"Oh, Madame." Nicole felt tears rush to her eyes.

"There's an inscription inside," Madame Preston said. "Go on, read it."

Nicole translated the French. "To my star pupil, may her future be bright."

"It was written to me, but it applies to you," Madame told her. "I know your future will be bright, Nicole. I've had good pupils before, but never with your heart. You'll always be special to me."

"Oh, Madame!" She couldn't speak. Instead she threw her arms around her teacher, and Madame Preston hugged her back. "I'll never have another teacher like you, either."

"I hope you'll get good use from that book, Nicole."

"I'm sure I will."

Madame Preston sighed. "Things won't be the same here without you."

Fondly Nicole looked around her old classroom, as if trying to memorize it. "I wonder if I'll ever be as comfortable in college as I was here."

"I think you will be," her teacher assured her. "Just give it some time."

"That's good advice," Nicole admitted. "Sometimes, I worry too much. In fact—" she hesitated— "I almost didn't go to Briarwood at all."

To her surprise she found herself telling Madame how she had panicked and applied to UCSB instead. The peculiar thing was, in telling Madame the story, it almost sounded funny. But just two days before, Nicole had been very serious.

"I really threw myself into applying to UCSB," she finished.

"Just like you." Madame laughed. "A hard worker, no matter what you do. Even if it's something foolish."

"I was pretty foolish," Nicole admitted, embarrassed. "But I was just so terrified of trying to make it on my own so far away from home. I guess I lost faith in myself," she said, recalling Bitsy's words. She ran her finger over the inscription inside the dictionary. "You must be disappointed in your star pupil."

"*Pas du tout*," Madame cried. "I'd have thought it strange if you *weren't* nervous. College is a big step, no matter where you go."

"I guess it is." Nicole began to feel a little better. If Madame didn't think she had gone off the deep end, maybe she needn't feel ashamed of herself.

"*Tu sais*, Nicole," Madame told her. "Many students transfer to other schools, and sometimes it's a very good thing to do. You must do what's right for you. Just make sure you give yourself a chance to decide calmly."

Nicole nodded gratefully. It helped to realize that she wasn't the first to panic or to think about changing schools. And it was good to know she had other options if she ever needed them.

As Madame began to talk over old times, Nicole found herself thinking again of her "bright future." It felt good to be excited about college. In fact, she felt better than she had in days! She was having such a good time talking with her teacher that she was startled to glance at the clock on the wall. "Look at the time," she exclaimed in surprise.

"Mon Dieu!" Using Nicole's favorite phrase, Madame Preston clapped a hand to her face. "I didn't realize it was so late."

Hastily she began gathering her things together. "I'm so sorry, Nicole—but I have an appointment downtown. Oh, I'll never make it." She gave a despairing glance at the textbooks strewn over the rows of desks where she had been examining them. "I have to straighten up in here and put things away!"

"You go on," Nicole said impulsively. "I'll finish here and lock up for you."

"Would you?"

Nicole nodded. "It's no problem. It's a thank-you from me."

Madame hesitated. "Well, okay. Here are the keys. Remember to leave them in the office, *oui*?"

"I will. You'd better go."

"I guess this is it then. *Bonne chance,* Nicole." Madame Preston gave Nicole one last hug. "And please write!"

"I will," Nicole called after her. Fondly she watched as her teacher hurried down the hall. With a sigh she turned back into the room. Then, dropping the keys on Madame Preston's desk, she began to stack the textbooks together and carry them into the walk-in storage closet at the back of the room.

"Well, that's the last of them," she finally said to herself, straightening the neat stacks. "Now, how does this lock work?"

Bending over, she examined the door. There was a keyhole in the doorknob on the outside of the storage closet, and a little button sticking out from the doorknob on the inside.

This looks easy enough, Nicole decided. She shut the door from inside the closet and pushed the little button so that it was flush with the doorknob. There was a satisfying click.

Good, Nicole thought. That works fine.

She turned the handle, expecting the button to pop out. It didn't budge.

"Mon Dieu." She shut her eyes. "It can't be!"

Trying to remain calm but with a terrible sinking feeling, Nicole tried the doorknob again. It didn't move. She'd made a terrible mistake. She'd locked the door from the inside, and now she couldn't get out!

Frantically she rattled the door, but it was tightly made and there was no give, not even space enough to stick a hairpin in the crack or somehow try to wedge it open. Besides, she wasn't wearing any hairpins, only combs, and they would snap if she tried such a thing.

Suddenly, it hit her—she was really stuck. Except for the janitor, whom she'd seen earlier down by the gym, the school was deserted. Madame had made a special trip in to see her new textbooks. No other teachers were there! Nicole yelled as loud as she could and pounded on the door anyway, but to no avail.

Feeling sick, she slowly sank down. What am I going to do? she wondered. I've got to get out of here. But no matter how hard she thought, she came up with nothing. There were no windows to break, no way to escape from the closet. She was doomed.

"*Idiote,*" she told herself angrily. Acting scared wouldn't help! Anyway, she knew her family would soon miss her. There really was no problem. Sooner or later someone would remember that Madame Preston had left a message for her last night—it was even written on her mother's note. Then they would put two and two together, and *voilà!* she'd be free.

Satisfied that her life wasn't in danger, Nicole suddenly began to feel foolish. What was wrong with her anyway? No sooner had she gotten out of one embarrassing mess than she got into another one.

"Calm down, Nicole," she ordered herself. "Getting angry won't help any more than getting scared. Someone is bound to find you eventually."

Chapter 14

Mollie thought the dinner looked wonderful. It had taken all day to prepare everything, but it was worth it. Only the finishing touches were left, and those could be done the instant they got home from Moveable Feasts. Mollie could hardly wait. In fact, she had already taken enough tastes during the day to satisfy her usually ravenous appetite—and to ruin her latest diet.

"It's beautiful, Mom," she said sincerely. "I can't believe we did it." She surveyed the table laden with food.

Cindy nodded in agreement. "Having you here made all the difference. Mollie and I actually cooked!"

"And cooked well," their mother added proudly.

"And cooking is not my strong point," Mollie said, grinning. "Or Cindy's, either."

Cindy pretended to scowl at her, but she knew that Mollie was telling the truth. Besides, they were both too happy to quarrel. The éclairs were a masterpiece, the chocolate mousse was setting in the cooler, and the coq au vin was assembled and ready for reheating at home. Even the salad had been put together, waiting only for a tossing with their mother's special dressing at home.

Laura Lewis checked her watch. "The guests are coming at five-thirty. An hour to go." She stacked the food containers together and handed them to her daughters. "You girls had better get going. You'll have to start decorating, and get the table set first thing."

"What about you?"

"I'll finish up here first. I'll be along a little later."

"Not too late," Mollie warned.

"In plenty of time to hide and yell 'surprise' when Nicole comes in."

"Okay. Do we do anything with the food?"

Their mother shook her head. "I'll heat things up and toss the salad after Nicole's surprise."

"Sounds perfect," Mollie declared. "Nothing can go wrong."

"Unless she drags Sean along," Cindy mumbled.

"She wouldn't," Mollie insisted. "He wasn't invited."

Cindy gave her a disparaging look. "Nicole doesn't know that. It's a surprise, remember? She has no idea there's a party."

"Oh, right." Mollie smiled guiltily. She had completely forgotten that no one knew that she had told Nicole about the surprise. She only hoped Nicole didn't bring Sean anyway. The way Nicole had been acting lately, she might do anything.

"Well, even if she does, there's plenty of food," Mollie pointed out.

"That's true, girls," their mother said. "No squabbling, now. Tonight has got to be a happy occasion."

"But what if Nicole comes in while we're setting up the table?"

"Yell 'surprise'?" Mollie asked innocently.

Cindy made a face at her sister.

"No," Mrs. Lewis said logically, "your father will be on the lookout. He said he'd be home from work early today. In fact, he should be there now. Whenever Nicole gets home, he's going to take her on a tour—to say good-bye to all her favorite places—until after five-thirty. Then he'll bring her home."

"A nostalgia tour, huh?" Cindy rolled her eyes. "Nicole should love that. She's the sentimental type."

At that moment, nostalgia was the last thing on Nicole's mind. She was frustrated and bored. Listlessly she flipped through one of the new textbooks.

Not too imaginative, she thought. If I were a teacher, I'd be more original. I'd do creative things to get my students interested, and I'd never make anyone memorize silly dialogues like these. Instead, I'd ... well ... Nicole thought hard. What *would* she do?

Write plays! She'd have the class write plays in French, and then act them out, using their new vocabulary. What a brilliant idea. It was so good, she decided to suggest it to Madame Preston in her first letter—maybe she would use the idea. Nicole could become famous—a famous French educator. She'd have a brilliant career and travel all over the world.

She settled against a stack of books and day-dreamed. She saw herself in Paris lecturing groups of visiting Americans. Everyone would look up to her and try to imitate her teaching methods. And Nicole would tell them all how she had almost missed her chance at a brilliant career, by not going to Briarwood. Luckily, she would say with a sigh, the story had a happy ending. . . .

Nicole sighed now. The story will have a happy ending if I ever get out of here.

Mollie pushed open the kitchen door. She and Cindy froze in alarm. "Dad! What are you doing here?" They peered behind him, looking for Nicole.

Mr. Lewis grinned amiably. "Where should I be?"

"Out—with Nicole." Mollie stared at him. "Didn't she come back yet?"

Behind her back, Mollie crossed her fingers. What if Nicole had told their father that she knew all about the surprise, that there was no need for him to drag her around town all afternoon to keep her away from the house?

But Mr. Lewis just shrugged. "The house has been empty since I got home from work about two hours ago. I've been watching for Nicole, but she hasn't shown up."

"Oh, no," Cindy groaned. "She *is* with Sean. Drat."

Secretly Mollie felt relieved. At least Nicole hadn't told on her yet.

"Well, no matter," Mr. Lewis said. "As long as

she's back in time for the party. But I'd better keep watch while you two get things set up."

"I guess."

They shut the door between the kitchen and dining room and propped a chair against it, so Nicole wouldn't be able to get through to the dining room. Then their father went to stand guard in the living room, while Cindy fetched the table-cloth and napkins and Mollie got out the good china and silverware. They had the table set in no time. For the final touch, Cindy brought in the basket of dried flowers. She and Mollie had already decided to pass the guest book around between dinner and dessert.

"I can't wait to see her face," Cindy bubbled. "Will she be surprised! She'll sure be in a good mood then."

"Uh, yeah." Busily Mollie moved the basket a little to the left so that it was exactly in the center of the table. Cindy would scream if she knew Nicole could only pretend to be surprised.

"Anyway," she said, glancing at the fresh food stains on her new sweatshirt, "if she's not sur-prised, I'll kill her." She had ruined the new shirt cooking the party dinner, and in Mollie's eyes that was punishment enough for spilling the beans. You could only take feeling guilty so far.

"That looks fine," Mr. Lewis said, admiring the dining room. He checked his watch and frowned. "Hmm—it's getting awfully late. I thought Nicole would be here by now."

"Still no sign of her?" Nervously, Mollie peered through the sheer dining room curtains. What was Nicole doing? She *knew* the party was for six o'clock. It was almost five-thirty now.

"Don't worry, Dad—she'll come in soon," she assured her father.

"I'm not really worried." He smiled. "Your mother told her not to make plans for tonight. Party or not, Nicole knows that she'd better be home."

"That's good," Mollie said uneasily.

Her father stretched. "Listen, girls, if she comes in now, keep her in the kitchen until I get down."

"Where are you going?" Mollie nearly shrieked.

"Upstairs. To freshen up. Don't be so nervous, Mollie."

Mollie smiled weakly.

"Yeah, shrimp," Cindy commented. "What are you so jumpy for?"

"No reason." She watched until her father was safely out of sight, up the stairs. "But, Cindy," she whispered, "I, uh, I think we should make some phone calls. Try to find Nicole. Maybe she's with Bitsy, and Bitsy could bring her over at six, when it's safe."

"Good idea," Cindy agreed.

Mollie waited nervously while Cindy dialed. "That's funny," Cindy said, hanging up. "Bitsy has no idea where Nicole is. But one thing," she added, "Bitsy was pretty sure Nicole broke up with Sean last night. So there's not much chance she's with him."

"There isn't?" Mollie bit her lip, but Cindy only shrugged.

"Oh, well. No problem. Like Dad said, she'll be home for dinner."

Mollie fidgeted. "Uh, Cindy—maybe we better talk."

"Sure. About what?"

Mollie's confession came out in a rush of words. "Nicole knows about the surprise. I told her."

Cindy gasped in disbelief.

"I couldn't help it," Mollie pleaded. "We were arguing, and it just kind of slipped out."

"That's great," Cindy muttered. "Why are we killing ourselves to surprise her? She won't be the least bit surprised."

"Mom and Dad don't know that, and neither do her friends," Mollie said.

"That's true. But it sure takes the fun out of it," Cindy complained.

Mollie grabbed her sister by the shoulders. "That's not the point. Think, Cindy—what if ... well, Nicole has been acting so strangely lately, what if she's trying to miss the party on purpose?"

"Why would she do that?"

"Who knows? Maybe she's mad at us. Maybe she's upset about Sean. Who knows anything about her anymore?"

Cindy stared at Mollie. "You may be right. What'll we do?"

"We've got to find her," Mollie said.

"But how?"

Mollie had no idea. Finally Cindy spoke up. "I know. You call Bitsy and tell her to call all Nicole's friends. If anyone sees Nicole anywhere, tell them to get her over here."

Mollie flew to the phone and reported back, "Bitsy's making the calls. Now what?"

Cindy bit her lip, thinking. "I don't know. We

can't sit here all night waiting. We've got to do something."

"This is just like her," Mollie fumed.

Cindy peered at her sister. "What are you so angry about? It's your fault she's missing. There's only one thing to do," she declared. "We'll have to look for her ourselves. Tell Dad. I'll get the car started."

Mollie soon joined Cindy in the family car. "We'll try all her old haunts," Cindy declared.

"It's almost funny," Mollie remarked. "Dad thought he'd take Nicole on a nostalgia trip, and instead, we're doing it."

"If you think that's funny, you have a pretty strange sense of humor." Cindy pulled onto the main road, trying to decide where to start. "Since she didn't have the car today, she either walked somewhere or rode her bicycle," she reasoned.

"That's one break," Mollie agreed. "Okay, then, we'll try everywhere within biking distance."

Cindy almost broke the speed limit, driving first to Miller's Cove, the tiny park on Cypress Lane, then to Taco Rio and Pete's Pizza, two of Nicole's favorite meeting places. But there was no sign of their sister.

Cindy made no attempt to cover up her feelings. "I'm furious with you, Mollie," she said. "If you hadn't told her, Nicole would be home by now."

"You don't know that," Mollie defended herself. "Besides, I'm furious with Nicole."

"How do you figure that?"

"Because she knows we're planning this dinner.

You'd think she'd try not to hurt everyone's feelings by missing her own going-away party."

"Forget it," Cindy said. "We've tried the cove, Taco Rio, Pete's Pizza, and all the local boutiques and galleries. She's nowhere!"

"She has to be someplace," Mollie argued. "What time is it?"

"Five-forty."

"Oh, no! Then people are already at the house."

"That's okay, shrimp. You have to come early to a surprise party, in time to hide and get ready to jump out. Really, it doesn't matter what time Nicole gets there now. As long as she gets there."

"That's easy for you to say. How long do you expect everyone to wait? They'll be hungry." Mollie put her hand on her own stomach, which grumbled loudly, as if on cue. If she hadn't been so upset about the ruined party, she would have laughed.

"Let's take one more drive in a circle," Cindy said. "Then I give up."

Mollie groaned. "It's all my fault," she fretted. "What if Nicole is doing this to me on purpose?"

Cindy almost felt sorry for her. "Next time, think before you talk," she scolded her sister.

"I know," Mollie grumbled, "but sometimes the words just come out and I don't even know where they come from."

Sighing, Cindy put the car in gear. "This is it," she declared. "One more drive around town, and then I'm heading home. I don't know what else we can do."

"Wait a minute," Mollie yelled. Her face broke into a smile. "Home—Nicole might be there already! She could have come home while we were out driving around. Let's call and find out."

"You're right," Cindy agreed. "Maybe they started the party without us!"

"Now who's jumping to conclusions?"

"Okay. Let's call. At least we won't be worried anymore." Cindy pulled over at the next pay phone and Mollie jumped out. Quickly she dialed her number. Her father answered.

"Dad—hi, it's me. No ... no luck here. We thought Nicole might be there already. I see." She covered the mouthpiece. "Everyone's there," she called to Cindy. "But no Nicole."

Cindy's shoulders sagged in discouragement.

"Okay, Dad, I will." Equally discouraged, Mollie came back to the car. "No sign of her."

"What did Dad say?"

"He said we should come right home. They can't think of anything to do but wait some more."

"This is a disaster," Cindy grumbled. "If only you hadn't told her, maybe none of this would have happened."

"I thought of that already. Thanks for making me feel even worse." Mollie scrunched down in the passenger seat.

But Mollie couldn't have felt worse than Nicole, who had given up on the idea of making the best of things. It was bad enough being stuck in the dusty old closet—but even worse to know she was holding up her own surprise party!

Nicole tried to pull herself together. Her excitement over her great teaching ideas hadn't lasted very long. She was trying to keep her mind on pleasant things, but it was difficult. Every ten minutes, like clockwork, she got up, banged on the door and yelled as loudly as she could.

But each time, nothing happened.

Why hadn't anyone come for her yet? How long did it take for them to realize she'd spent the afternoon with Madame Preston? What on earth were they waiting for? She could die in this closet—they'd find her bones when school started in a few weeks.

Stop it! she told herself firmly. She was only scaring herself. That was no good. As calmly as possible, Nicole sat down to wait until the next ten minutes had gone by. If only someone would rescue her!

Chapter 15

"*C*indy . . ." *Mollie nudged her sister gently.* "Hey, the light is green. You can go." Cindy didn't respond. "Hello? Anybody there?"

Cindy's eyes widened. "I just had this crazy idea . . . No, it couldn't be."

"What?"

"Well, it's just an idea, but . . . what if Nicole went to see Madame Preston today? Didn't Mom say that she called last night?"

Mollie nodded thoughtfully. "It's worth a try."

"Okay, but I don't know where she lives. Do you?"

"No, but we can call."

"Great." Cindy made a U-turn and pulled up at the telephone again. Mollie leaped out. As Cindy watched, she got Madame Preston's number from the operator and quickly dialed it. Cindy waited impatiently, tapping on the steering wheel. In a flash Mollie was back in the car, her cheeks flushed and a puzzled look on her face.

"Well? What happened? Did you get her? What'd she say? Has she seen Nicole?"

"Yes and no. She did see her at the high school. But that was hours ago."

"Oh." Cindy began tapping the steering wheel again. "Well, maybe she's still there. You know how much Nicole loved school."

"Not even Nicole liked school that much," Mollie remarked.

Cindy nodded in agreement, but didn't turn the car around to head home.

"Except ..." Mollie said slowly.

"What?"

Mollie hesitated, "Well, Madame Preston did say Nicole stayed after, to straighten up the classroom. Maybe ..."

"Look—it's a lost cause," Cindy said, "but let's swing by the high school. It's worth a try."

"That's crazy," Mollie declared.

"I know, but I have this weird feeling. . . ."

"But what would she be doing there for so long?"

"Who knows?" Cindy shrugged helplessly. "If it were anyone else, I'd say it was a pretty dumb idea. But this is Nicole we're talking about."

"Yeah." Mollie giggled for the first time since their search had begun. "Maybe she's in her old classroom, conjugating verbs."

"Okay," Cindy decided, "we'll give it a try."

They drove in silence, each of them lost in her own thoughts. "Look," Mollie screamed, "there's her bike!"

Cindy parked the car in the school parking lot, and they raced to the bicycle rack.

"Our first clue," Mollie cried. She scanned the schoolyard. It was empty, and the school was dark.

"We have to get in," Cindy said desperately. "She's in there, I know it. She has to be."

Mollie looked at her sister. Neither of them said anything, but they were both thinking the same thing. If Nicole wasn't in the school, then something terrible might have happened to her!

They banged on the front doors for what seemed an eternity. Finally, a janitor appeared. "Go away, school's closed," he shouted, waving them away.

Cindy and Mollie screamed explanations through the closed doors, babbling about lost sisters and surprise parties, and by the time the janitor unlocked the doors, he looked as anxious as they did.

"Oh, thank you," Mollie gushed. "We've just got to find our sister."

"Come on, Mollie, let's go check Madame Preston's room," Cindy said, heading straight for the stairwell.

"I'll search the first floor," the janitor offered.

Cindy and Mollie sped down the deserted halls. The empty school seemed huge and eerie, and it seemed to take ages to get to Madame Preston's classroom.

"It's empty," Mollie wailed. "Oh, no! Now what?" She collapsed against the classroom door.

"Look—Nicole's pocketbook!" Cindy rushed to the desk and grabbed it. It dangled from her fist.

"But where's Nicole?" Mollie turned pale. "What if she's been kidnapped, or—" Mollie bolted from the room. "We've got to find her."

"Wait!" In the corridor, Cindy grabbed Mollie's arm. "What's that noise?"

"I don't hear anything."

"Shh! Yes—someone's banging. Listen!"

Eyes wide, they both rushed back inside the classroom.

"It's coming from the closet! Nicole? Nicole!"

"Mollie! Cindy!" The tears Nicole had been holding back all day suddenly spilled out. She pounded on the closet door, sobbing with relief. "In here! In the closet! The key is on the desk."

Cindy whirled. "I see it!" With shaking hands, Cindy grabbed the key and sprang to the closet door, fitting the key into the lock. The door opened and Nicole fell out, embracing both her sisters.

"Cindy! Mollie! Thank goodness. I thought I'd die in there! Where were you?"

"Where were *we*?" Cindy stared at her sister in disbelief.

"Trying to find you," Mollie cried. "We didn't know what to do!"

"We were frantic," Cindy said. "We looked everywhere, called everyone, but no one knew where you were. Finally we remembered that message from Madame Preston, so we called her."

"Thank goodness you did. Oh, Cindy." Nicole leaned against her sister. "It was awful."

"But what happened? How'd you get in the closet?"

Nicole swallowed deeply and confessed that she had locked herself in. "Pretty dumb, huh?"

Mollie stared at her, wide-eyed. "You did that? I can't believe it."

"Why not?" Nicole laughed weakly. "I've done a lot of dumb things lately."

"Well, don't worry about it," Mollie told her. "I'm just glad we found you and you're okay."

Cindy agreed. "But I was furious with you, Nicole."

"You were? Why?"

"We thought you were doing it on purpose."

Nicole stared. "Doing what?"

"Hiding out," Mollie replied. "Avoiding your party, because I spilled the beans. And you were so mad at us anyway."

"Mad at you?" Baffled, Nicole sat down at the nearest desk. "Why would I be mad at you?"

Mollie and Cindy exchanged unbelieving looks. "We don't know. But you were sure acting weird."

"Oh. *Je sais.*" Nicole stared down at the tiled floor. "I guess I have been acting horrible lately."

Mollie rolled her eyes. "Tell me about it."

"But I didn't mean to. It was just ... well, I was so anxious and worried about going away to school, and I guess I was afraid to admit it."

Astounded, Mollie and Cindy stared at their sister.

"You?" Mollie's blue eyes opened wide. "You were worried?"

"I'm human, too," Nicole said defensively. "College is a big step, and I was nervous. And there's nothing wrong with that," she added, remembering what Madame Preston had said.

"I know that," Mollie said. "I get nervous all the time. But not you ..."

"You always do everything right," Cindy agreed. "I thought nothing ever bothered you."

"Plenty of things bother me," Nicole admitted. "Like thinking no one at home was going to miss me."

"Huh? Why would you think that?"

Nicole raised her head defiantly. "Because that's how you both acted. Cindy, all you cared about was getting the car! You couldn't wait for me to leave. And, Mollie, you just wanted all my old clothes. Even Mother turned down my offer to help manage Moveable Feasts. I felt as if no one wanted me around." Nicole wiped her eyes. Her string of complaints had brought back all the pain she'd been feeling.

Her sisters looked dumbfounded. "But, Nicole," Mollie protested, "I was just trying to help. I thought you couldn't wait to get away from *me*."

"Me, too," Cindy confessed. "I felt like I was in *your* way, and you couldn't wait to get to school."

"*Mon Dieu*," Nicole cried, "everyone was all wrong! I didn't want to go! I even ..." She flushed. Should she tell the whole truth? "I even considered not going away to school at all," she admitted. "And ... and Sean helped me apply to UCSB, just in case."

"That explains it," Cindy said thoughtfully. "I couldn't figure you and Sean together. But that makes sense." She chuckled. "I can't imagine your staying here. I mean, we'll all miss you, but you've talked about going to Briarwood for so long, I couldn't think of you at any other college."

"Me, either," Mollie said. "It wouldn't seem

right. And this way Cindy and I will get to visit you in Massachusetts. Besides, you love the place already."

"I guess I do," Nicole agreed. "Bitsy said I had a case of leaving-home jitters. I guess she was right."

"But you're better now?" Mollie asked.

"All better," Nicole said, getting up. She swung her pocketbook over her shoulder. "And I guess we should be going."

"You're right," Cindy exclaimed. "Everyone is already at the house waiting for us. Mom and Dad will be frantic."

"We'd better find the janitor who let you in, to tell him I'm safe," Nicole said, feeling more her old self again. "Though I feel awfully foolish."

"Don't worry about that," Mollie assured her, thinking of Richie and her own narrow escape from an embarrassing situation. "Everyone acts foolish sometimes."

"Very wise, shrimp," Cindy said approvingly. She glanced at her watch. "Hey, if we really hustle, we can make it back to the house in plenty of time for Nicole to act surprised."

"I've already been surprised," Nicole told them. "My surprise was in finding out how much I would miss you all. Mom and Dad and all my friends—and of course my two sisters. No matter what, you guys are the best friends I'll ever have."

Cindy hugged Nicole, and Mollie threw her arms around both of them. "I really messed up this week," Nicole confessed. "But I'm glad I found out how much you'll really miss me."

"Of course we'll miss you," Cindy assured her, trying to hide her watery eyes.

"I know it's crazy, because I really do want to go away to school," Nicole added. "But, *mon Dieu*, if I could stay here with the two of you, I'd do it."

Mollie wiped a tear off her own cheek. "That wouldn't be very sensible," she declared.

Squeezing both her sisters very hard, Nicole happily agreed.

Here's a sample of what awaits you in AND THEN THERE WERE TWO, book fifteen in the "Sisters" series for GIRLS ONLY.

"Mollie's coming to the beach specially to hang out with us?" Grant MacPhearson asked Cindy later as they sat side by side on the gang's beach blanket. Grant had been dating Cindy for just about a year now and was very familiar with the huge differences between the Lewis sisters.

Cindy looked into Grant's puzzled blue-green eyes, then glanced around the blanket to find all her friends reeling from her announcement. "I know it seems strange . . ."

"I'll say," Carey remarked. "Mollie usually comes to the beach to chase guys, not waves."

"Is she trying to sell us something?" Anna wondered aloud.

Duffy shook his bright red head. "Those fluorescent lights in the stores have finally fried the super shopper's brain!"

"Mollie's going through a rough time right now," Cindy explained as she rubbed some bright pink zinc oxide on her nose. "She's missing Nicole a lot and to top it all off, she says her friends don't understand her anymore . . ." Cindy trailed off, flashing Duffy a hopeful expression.

"What are you looking at me for?" Duffy demanded.

"I hope you'll control your wisecracks, Duffy," Cindy said, accustomed to being blunt with her rambunctious childhood friend. "Mollie's pretty sensitive right now."

"Give me a break, Lewis," Duffy shot back. "I'm a nice guy."

His last remark caused gales of laughter to erupt on the crowded beach blanket.

"Here comes the Lewis mobile," Grant observed, pointing to the parking lot. Moments later the Lewis's station wagon rolled to a stop on the blacktop and Mollie hopped out of the passenger side of the car dressed in a purple terry cloth sunsuit, her long blond hair gathered up in a pony tail, and huge sunglasses perched on her nose. Cindy immediately jumped up and began to wave her arms in the air to attract Mollie's attention. Mollie waved back and began to scamper across the sand toward them.

"Hi, everybody!" Mollie greeted the group brightly, sitting down on the only open corner of the blanket. "Looks like a lot of awesome waves out there," she observed in an effort to sound like part of the surfer crowd.

"Very very awesome," Duffy agreed.

"They close the mall for repairs?" Grant asked with a devilish grin.

"I was there this morning and the building was in pretty good shape," Mollie tossed back lightly, determined to show them how nice and fun she could be.

"I figured you'd wear a swimsuit," Cindy said in surprise.

"I don't feel like swimming today," Mollie explained. "I just thought I'd stop by to hang out with the best juniors at Vista High for a while."

Mollie's compliment hit its mark, bringing smiles to everyone's lips.

"You've got some real sense for a sophomore," Duffy said.

"You're wearing a cute outfit, Mollie," Anna complimented.

Cary nodded. "Purple is a good color on you."

Mollie glowed under their praise, struggling not to appear too eager. She wondered why she'd never bothered with Cindy's friends before. They really were nice.

"When are you going to ride your first curl, Mollie?" Grant asked, reaching into the Lewis's cooler for a sandwich.

"Catch a wave and you're sittin' on top of the world," Duffy chimed in.

"Curl. Wave. Sounds like beauty salon talk," Mollie said.

"Take that back or I'll bury you in the sand," Duffy threatened.

"I'm only kidding," Mollie hastened to assure them. "As a matter of fact, I figure it's about time I learn to surf."

The crowd didn't bother to hide their amazement.

"But Mollie," Cindy objected. "Surfing isn't as easy as it looks."

Mollie brushed aside her sister's objection with a carefree hand. "I can handle it, Cindy—if you're willing to teach me, that is."

Cindy looked into Mollie's anxious blue eyes and all of her arguments melted away. "All right. We'll give it a shot next weekend."

Cindy was surrounded with good humored, but skeptical looks.

"This is going to work out great," Mollie enthused, pushing her glasses up on her nose. She had never thought she'd have a better time at the beach than she did at the mall!

28   JOB-2